# The Wereling

# Wounded

# The Wereling

BY
STEPHEN COLE

## BOOK ONE

# WOUNDED

raz**O**r
**bill**
NEW YORK

The Wereling: Wounded

RAZORBILL

Published by the Penguin Group
Penguin Young Readers Group
345 Hudson Street, New York, New York 10014, U.S.A.
Penguin Group (USA) Inc., 375 Hudson Street, New York,
New York 10014, U.S.A
Penguin Books Canada Ltd, 10 Alcorn Avenue, Toronto,
Ontario, Canada M4V 3B2 (a division of Pearson Penguin Canada, Inc.)
Penguin Books Ltd, 80 Strand, London WC2R 0RL, England
Penguin Ireland, 25 St Stephen's Green, Dublin 2, Ireland
(a division of Penguin Books Ltd)
Penguin Group (Australia), 250 Camberwell Road, Camberwell,
Victoria 3124, Australia (a division of Pearson Australia Group Pty Ltd)
Penguin Books India Pvt Ltd, 11 Community Centre,
Panchsheel Park, New Delhi – 110 017, India
Penguin Group (NZ), Cnr Airborne and Rosedale Roads, Albany,
Auckland 1310, New Zealand (a division of Pearson New Zealand Ltd)
Penguin Books (South Africa) (Pty) Ltd, 24 Sturdee Avenue,
Rosebank, Johannesburg 2196, South Africa

Penguin Books Ltd, Registered Offices: 80 Strand,
London WC2R 0RL, England

10 9 8 7 6 5 4 3 2 1

Originally published in the United Kingdom by Bloomsbury Publishing Plc,
38 Soho Square, London, W1D 3HB

Library of Congress Cataloging-in-Publication Data

Cole, Stephen, 1971–
  Wounded / by Stephen Cole.
    p. cm. — (The wereling ; bk. 1)
  Summary: Sixteen-year-old Tom Anderson and seventeen-year-old Kate Folan
try to escape Kate's werewolf family—and fight becoming werewolves
themselves—by making a cross-country journey in search of a mysterious man
who might have a cure.
  ISBN 1-59514-041-7 (pbk.)
  [1. Werewolves—Fiction. 2. Travel—Fiction. 3. Horror stories.]  I. Title.
II. Series: Cole, Stephen, 1971–    Wereling ; v bk. 1.
  PZ7.C67356Wo 2005
  [Fic]—dc22

                                                          2004018262

Printed in the United States of America

*To John Leonard Smith*

# PROLOGUE

It's late. The moon, full and fat, is blinding bright through the window above Kate Folan's bed. It's not a comforting light. It only makes the wide night sky seem even blacker.

Kate can feel it through the glass, bathing her sweating skin like ice water.

She's so hot.

She leans over and heaves open the window. Her shaky breath mists out and mingles with the thick night air. She lifts the damp, dark hair from the back of her neck to expose it to the cool breeze.

So many scents and sounds carry in from outside. . . .

There's a tiny electric buzz sparking in her bones. It tickles and warms her, as if her whole body is itching on the inside and she has no way to scratch. It's maddening. Dizzying.

Kate shuts her eyes, shakes her head. She wants to let go. To lose the fear and the doubts—just give

1

in to the craving. Why should she fight it? This *has* to happen. . . .

Kate's heart begins to pound. It feels like a fist knocking against her ribs, so hard it hurts. She can see its movement beneath the soaked white cotton of her nightclothes.

The moon seems incandescent, like it has caught fire.

Kate knows now. It will happen tonight.

The burning heat now pounding through her body seems to be melting her bones. The pain is delicious, irresistible. Kate wonders how she could ever have wished it away.

The change feels maddeningly near now. Why won't it come?

Kate clutches the bedclothes, panting for breath, filling her lungs with the scents of the night. She could howl with pain and frustration.

*So* close . . .

She bites her lip, tastes the iron tang of her own blood—then smiles as, under the moon's gaze, spasms of sheer exhilaration shoot through her.

It has begun.

Kate laughs feverishly as her bones begin to shift. Muscles tear and ripple. Teeth twist into spikes. Silken hair sprouts from every sweating pore. She shucks off her damp, clinging clothes, rolls over onto her front, then giddily raises herself from the bed.

Her heart beats sure and strong. This room, these things, these meaningless possessions, none of them are hers. All she owns is the night world outside—and everything in it.

She leaps through the window onto the roof outside, then down to the grassy field leading into the wood. She glories in her speed, her agility.

Soon she is bounding over rich-smelling earth. At last she feels alive. Feels she belongs. She catches the sharp smell of a frightened animal close by. She slips through undergrowth toward it. A deer, startled, bursts from its hiding place and starts to bolt. She matches it for pace, watches it swerve and dance with fear.

Finally she tires of the chase and slams the animal to the ground. Her claws tear into the deer's flank; her jaws close around its throat, sharp teeth piercing the downy neck. Blood floods over her lips. It's everywhere, sweet and sticky; she is bathed in it. Exultant, she raises her head and howls her thanks to the moon. . . .

The scream tore out of Kate as her eyes snapped open.

She jolted upright in her bed, trembling, gasping for air. She pressed her hands to her face, fingers searching the smooth clammy skin as hot tears poured over them. Then she gagged. The dream had never been so vivid; the blood had never seemed so real.

The moon was just a soft glow through her flimsy curtains, but Kate feared even that intrusion. She pushed sweat-drenched hair from her eyes and turned on her bedside light. Looking around at the familiar objects in the room, she reassured herself she was normal. For now . . .

But the images of the dream wouldn't fade this time. The moon. The blood.

The exultant wolf.

*That's going to be me,* she thought, still trembling. *That's what I'm going to become.*

Kate dreaded the day she would think those thoughts not with fear and guilt and shame—but with pleasure. . . .

# CHAPTER ONE

The forest was silent and still, the hush almost expectant. Like the place was waiting for something to happen.

Tom Anderson shivered as he stood there in the crisp morning air. He zipped up his hooded sweatshirt, then pressed on through the sprawling spruces and towering pines. They stood untouched by fall's orange fingers. Their cold Christmas smell filled his head. The trees scratched at him and scattered needles as he left the trail to push farther into the thick undergrowth.

Moments later Tom stopped again. It was crazy, but he couldn't help feeling there was something in the forest, lurking just out of view. Watching him. He looked all around him. Everything remained still.

The silence began to creep Tom out, so he crashed on noisily. Just so there was something to hear. *Well, that's lame,* he thought as he struggled through a tangle of vines into a clearing. *Been watching too many late-night movies.* But he looked again for any trace of movement in the trees and bushes, just in case.

The thought that he was the one who had stalked out on his family, complaining about needing alone time, only made him more irritated. Snatches of conversation came back to him as he walked on.

His mom, pleading. "I know you're sixteen now, Tom, but you can go camping with your friends next year, honey. Just one more family vacation, okay?"

His dad, red faced and scowling. "One last family vacation. That was the deal, remember? You know this means a lot to your mom."

His little brother, Joe. "You never want to hang out with me these days, Tom. You're just no fun anymore."

His buddy Corey, shaking his head in sympathy. "So your parents really are making you go on vacation with them? You poor loser."

Finally, himself. This morning. Stomping out of the rented cabin in the Seattle hills. Slamming the door behind him. "Seven days stuck here is going to drive me crazy!"

Tom felt a twinge of guilt. He knew his mom would be upset again. He knew his dad would be calming her down right now, telling her it was okay. He'd be spouting the usual garbage about Tom being at a "difficult age." That one really ate at Tom.

What was "difficult" was having no time and space to himself! Hell, at sixteen he should have a little independence!

Right now, his friends would be camping out at Yosemite, having a real vacation. Tom was missing out on that for a week of being the obedient son.

A twig cracked underfoot, sounding like a rifle shot. Tom's heart thudded. He looked quickly around, half expecting the sound to have brought something out of hiding.

But nothing moved.

The sun began to emerge from behind the billowy clouds overhead. Tom felt its warm touch on his skin. Pushing away his thoughts, he pressed on along a winding path. Somewhere ahead of him a welcome noise whispered into the silence: the rushing and gurgling of fast-running water.

"You'll love the river," his father had promised him on the long drive from Denver. "Me and Gramps used to make camp there when I was a kid. It's some sight."

Tom had just yawned. "Sure, Dad. A river. Awesome."

Now, as Tom followed the sound, it grew louder and throatier. Finally it led him into a leafy glade, drenched with sunshine. A sloping shelf of mud led down to the riverbank. White light sparkled in the clear waters speeding past. Tom smiled. "Okay, Dad," he said aloud. "So maybe you were right."

It *was* a pretty awesome sight. The chill had gone from the air, and the walk had left Tom hot and sweaty. The water looked too good to resist.

"But you can't go swimming there," his dad had continued. "The current's too strong. Drags you down into the rapids. You'd never escape," he'd warned.

Tom hesitated, listening to the roar of the water. Now that the river had dared break the silence in the forest, he felt more confident. He wouldn't swim. But he could try a little wading. It wouldn't be so bad in the shallows. Then he'd go back to the cabin and tell Dad about how the old river had worked its magic, just as it had on him and Gramps. Dad would be pleased and Mom would forget about all the arguing.

He kicked off his Nikes, stripped off his sweatshirt and jeans, and scrambled down the bank. Maybe he'd bring Joe to the river later.

The water was dark up close. Tom drew a sharp breath; then, eager to get the shock of the cold over with, he splashed quickly into the river.

When he was up to his middle, he crouched down, whooping as the water closed over his shoulders. He grinned and shivered. Then he shut his eyes, held his nose, and sank his head beneath the shimmering surface.

It was a shame Joe wasn't here. Tom felt a pang. Joe was right: Tom hadn't had much time for him lately. He and Joe had always played this game whenever they went to the swimming pool. Sinking in the water like stones. Enjoying the weird way sound filtered through the water. Feeling the pressure in their heads. Seeing how long they could hold their breath.

Suddenly Tom heard something. A kind of muffled roaring sound, carried to him by the murky ripples of the river. At first he thought it was just the pressure of his lungs wanting air, the dizzying rush of blood thundering in his temples. But the noise got louder—somehow angry, threatening.

The clear water began to churn rhythmically around him. Something was approaching.

Tom burst up choking from the surface of the river. He wiped his dark hair back from his eyes, blinking rapidly as he tried to get his bearings.

The roar came again, low and guttural. Terrified, Tom groped blindly for the riverbank, tumbling forward through the water.

Something was wrong—the river was getting deeper, not shallower. At last his eyes cleared. He was looking into the center of the river. He twisted his body around to face the bank.

Big mistake.

Towering above him on its hind legs, barring his way back to safety, was the massive bulk of a full-grown grizzly bear. Its dark fur, silver at the tips, was sleek and wet. Its jaws gaped wide open as it bellowed in anger. Huge arms reached out for him. Daggerlike claws scythed the air.

Tom stared around wildly for some kind of

escape route. There was none. The bear roared again, powering its heavy frame through the water toward him. Tom panicked and backed away. He must have disturbed the thing at its fishing grounds or something. Wasn't fishing something bears did? He tried to focus, clear his rush of thoughts, but the water was up to his chin now. Only one fact about bears came resoundingly to mind.

*They're omnivores. They eat anything.*

The creature lunged forward, its huge body bearing down on him. Tom fell backward at the same moment as he lost his footing on the rocky riverbed. He launched into an awkward backstroke, splashing up at the bear with his feet and shouting to try to scare it off.

The animal watched and snarled, but it didn't try to follow. Tom felt relief surge through his shivering body. Then he froze mid-stroke as he felt the current coiling around his arms and legs, dragging him away.

*"The current's too strong,"* Dad had told him. *"You'd never escape."*

Tom cursed himself. The bear had only let him go because it knew these waters better than he did. Bracing himself, Tom launched into a powerful crawl, aiming for the far side of the bank. It was only fifty yards or so.

His arms windmilled until they cramped, but he found the bank was getting farther away, not nearer. He was being tugged downriver.

*". . . drags you down into the rapids."*

Tom saw the huge form of the bear dwindle to a dark speck and the glade vanish from view entirely. Then his head dipped underwater as the river picked up speed. Frantically he kicked his legs, trying to keep afloat, but it was impossible to keep upright now. Tree branches dangled temptingly overhead. He bobbed up with arms outstretched, desperately grabbing for one. Fir needles grazed his fingers but slipped from his grip. The sky spun crazily above him as the water whirled and foamed, dragging him under again and again. Each time Tom's head reached above water, he gulped for air.

Then all the breath was slammed from his body as the current swept him into a massive rock. Choking on water, Tom realized the rapids were just getting started. He tumbled past one more huge rock, worn smooth and round. He reached for it clumsily but was going too quickly now to hold on. He was still reaching out for the boulder when he smashed his head against another. The world turned red as blood washed into his eyes. The current was dizzying; he was a rag doll helpless in the grip of a whirlpool. Head pounding, too weak to resist any longer, Tom felt himself going down for the last time.

For a few moments he was sure he must be dead. Then sensation began to creep cruelly back into his body. It felt like someone was holding a blowtorch to his freezing skin. His legs cramped up like his muscles had been slammed in a vise, and he cried out. He was alive, all right. Death could never hurt as much as this. A trickle of blood ran down his cheek from a cut above his eye.

He reached for his calves, trying to rub the muscles into unclenching. Where was he? How long had he been lying there? Many hours. It was dark. The moon was full and heavy in the sky, like a huge boulder about to drop and crush him.

Thick mud slurped at his shoulders. He was lying in shallow water. Farther out, he could hear the foaming rapids.

How far down the river had he drifted? Tom surveyed the rushing water, straining his eyes to catch details in the dim light. A little way upstream a line of stones stuck out of the water like a row of bald heads. They acted as a kind of breakwater. If he'd been knocked into one and then pushed behind the line . . . Yeah, that was it. The gentler current had then carried him here to the river's edge.

Tom took a deep, shuddering breath. He'd made it. He'd had an unbelievable adventure, but he'd made it. Through the pain, through the shock—or maybe because of it—Tom found himself laughing.

Until something growled behind him.

His first thought was that the bear had somehow found him again. But the growl seemed somehow . . . *different*. Too exhausted to turn around, Tom let his head fall back. He had a crazy upside-down view of the gloomy riverbank, and his weary brain fought to make sense of it.

A stretch of slimy mud. A tangle of vegetation. Weird, misshapen tree roots reaching out deformed fingers. Two narrowed yellow eyes, glinting, low down in the shadows.

The eyes came closer and the shadows seemed to swallow him whole.

# CHAPTER TWO

*"How're you doing?"*

Tom could barely hear the voice. He was back in the cold freezing water, deep down and drowning.

*"C'mon, wake up, huh? Hey, what's your name?"*

Why should he wake up? He knew he would start hurting all over again if he woke up; if he let himself be dragged back to life. But the water was growing warmer already and thickening, until it felt more like blood.

Tom shook his head, moaned softly. As his body began to thaw out, he felt the pain creeping back into his muscles.

*"You've been asleep for ages."*

The blackness was melting into blues and purples, a swelling bruise over his vision. Tom's body started to thud, like the echoes of a giant's footsteps were hammering on him. He felt sick. He wanted to go back into the cold, numb darkness.

Except now he knew. In the darkness something was waiting for him.

He jolted fully awake, feeling an urge to scream—and glimpsed anxious faces he didn't recognize, watching him.

The darkness reached out for him again.

Tom was dimly aware of time passing. Of the moon and the sun switching places in his view outside. Of hands that spooned a bitter-tasting liquid into his dry mouth and rubbed a pungent lotion into his stinging skin.

Maybe he was in a hospital. *That must be it,* he decided. He had a fever and he was in a hospital room somewhere.

At last he worked up the courage to open his eyes and look around him. An almost-full moon glowed in the dark square of a window opposite him. It seemed like an accusing eye, looking in at him. Unable to meet its gaze, Tom turned away.

Through the gloom he saw that he was lying in a narrow bed in a narrow room. An open door gave onto a tiny bathroom. The only other furniture was the dark bulk of a dressing table and mirror lurking in the shadows against the wall.

The rattle of a key turning in a lock made Tom look up. He blinked as three figures entered the room: a man, a woman, and a boy around Tom's own age.

"You're awake!" remarked the woman with satisfaction. "I mean, really awake!"

Tom took in her gaunt face, framed by straight, dark hair. He didn't think he recognized her—or the others.

She came closer, out of the shadows. Her eyes were a cool blue, but her smile seemed warm. "We've been worried about you, young man. Very worried."

"Are you a nurse?" Tom croaked.

"Used to be," the woman said briskly, peering at Tom's bandages. "Used to be a *senior* nurse, at that."

"So I'm not in the hospital?" Tom asked nervously.

"Better than that," the woman assured him. "You're with friends." She fluffed up his pillow. "Hospitals are such unhealthy places, anyway. The bigger they are, the less they care. That's not the kind of nursing I like." She smiled at him again. "Marcie Folan. How do you do?" She held out a hand.

"My name's Tom." He tried to raise his own hand but found it wrapped heavily in bandages. He stared at it in confusion.

"Tom," echoed Marcie, as if she was trying the name on for size. Then she clicked her tongue sympathetically and lowered her hand. "I'm sorry, Tom. I was only fooling with you. No handshakes for you for a while. Not for a long while."

Tom realized that his legs and face were also swathed in bandages and dressings. He groaned.

The man stepped forward now, a faint smile on

his lips. He was about forty, with close-cropped graying hair and a well-groomed beard. "How're you feeling, son?"

"Okay," Tom said, swallowing thickly.

"Good," said the boy. He sat on the end of the bed and grinned, running a hand through his spiky reddish hair. "You've been out of it for ages."

"Oh . . . was it you who was calling to me?" Tom asked.

The boy nodded. "I'm Wes," he informed Tom.

"And I'm Henry, Wesley's father," the man added. "You can call me Hal."

"So," asked Wes, still smiling. "Tom what?"

"Anderson. Tom Anderson," Tom replied.

Marcie Folan unwrapped some fresh bandages. "Well, Tom Anderson, you must be some swimmer to get through those rapids."

Tom winced as Marcie eased the stained dressings away from his sore knuckles. "What happened to me? How did I get here?" He frowned. "Where *is* here?"

Hal was still watching him intently. "You're on our island."

Tom stared back, eyes wide. "You have your own *island?*"

"Uh-huh," said Wes. "Great place to live—but it can be a drag when the causeway is flooded and you're stuck here." He grinned, then shot a glance at his mother, as if wondering what to say next.

Marcie nodded encouragingly.

"It was lucky I found you," Wes went on. "You were unconscious and bleeding on the bank."

Everyone looked at Tom solemnly, as if this had somehow been his fault.

"I think I remember . . ." Tom croaked. "There was a bear, or . . ."

*The creature rushed for him, jaws snapping—*

Tom shuddered, unable to continue. He shook his head to try to clear it.

Wes's pale gray eyes were wide. "Yeah, there were some tracks in the mud near where we found you. We went out hunting for whatever it was," he said. "But there was no sign. Must have headed back to the mainland before the floods."

"Floods?" Tom looked at him blankly.

"It's been raining heavily these past three days," Marcie told him as she wrapped clean dressings around his arms.

Tom shut his eyes, felt his head throb as he tried to process all this information. "I've been here *three* days?" he asked incredulously. "What about my mom and dad? They must be freaking out."

"Sorry, honey." Marcie gave him a small, sympathetic smile. "As Wes said, the island's cut off when the causeway is flooded. And we have no phone line here. We haven't been able to get in touch with anyone."

"But . . ." Tom struggled up in bed. "Don't you have a cell phone?"

Hal Folan shook his head. "Sorry. We chose this place as a retreat from the outside world. A *total* retreat. Anyway, there are no cell phone towers for miles."

Marcie patted Tom's arm reassuringly. "Don't worry, honey. As soon as those floods clear, we'll get you right back to your family. Promise." She smiled again. "And in the meantime, I'm here to make sure you get well."

Tom looked at his bandaged hands and wrists. "Did an animal do this to me?"

"No," Marcie replied. "That was just bad luck. You got tangled up in some belladonna."

Tom frowned. "I did what?"

"Deadly nightshade," Hal explained. "You must've hauled yourself out of the water, pulling on the roots. Pretty toxic stuff; got in through the cuts on your hands."

Tom let his head sink back on the pillow. "I just don't remember." He sighed.

Marcie placed a cool hand on his burning forehead. "Just relax, Tom. My herbal cures have been fixing you up. Better than any drugs a hospital can give you." She nodded decisively. "And I should know, right?"

"Right," Tom replied wearily. "Thanks," he added. "Really. Thank you for looking after me."

"The pleasure's all ours," Marcie assured him. She looked at the others. "Right, boys?"

Hal and Wes both smiled at him.

Tom tried to smile back, but he felt his eyelids drooping. As he gave up and let the blackness come for him again, he could feel Marcie Folan still close by, a shifting shadow.

That night Tom had a nightmare.

He was running. The dark, barren landscape was flat under a sky that flickered like flames. The endless plain offered no shelter. No hiding place. And something was coming for him. Something that knew the darkness well, that loved it. Thrived on it.

Something evil and all-possessing that wanted him.

Yellow eyes watched him run. They shone. Tom felt them on his back. Like a laser sight on a rifle, marking him for death. Long bony jaws snapped. A hiss of triumph sounded from behind him, just out of view. He felt hot breath on the back of his neck. A roaring, rushing noise began to rise up around his ears.

Tom awoke just as the creature's teeth were closing on his flesh. He sat upright in his bed, wide awake, drenched in sweat. The noise was his frantic breathing.

Through the window the sun was heaving itself over the horizon. His sheets were coiled around him like fat white snakes.

The key rattled in the lock and Marcie glided

into the room in a long nightgown, her dark hair mussed up from sleep. "We heard a noise," she said. "Bad dreams?"

Tom shuddered, his heart still racing wildly. "The worst," he whispered.

Marcie smiled. "Well, if that was the worst, your dreams can only get better from now on, right, honey?" She poured thick syrup from a large brown bottle into a glass and handed it to Tom. "And they will. You'll see. You tell yourself that before this sends you back to sleep, okay?"

Tom took the glass and drained it. It had an odd sweet burning taste, like aniseed.

Marcie busied herself rearranging the bedclothes.

As Tom started drifting back to sleep, he heard raised voices from outside the room. A man shouting—Hal?—and what sounded like a girl's voice yelling back at him. He tried to catch the angry words, but Marcie's concoction was knocking him sideways. He couldn't focus on anything. "Who's that?" he drawled, his vision beginning to blur. "The girl, I mean . . ."

"You'll find out," Marcie promised him. "But not today," she added as she faded from Tom's view.

## CHAPTER THREE

"Wake up. Wake *up*."

Tom woke to find Wesley Folan sitting on his bed. Thin, watery light filtered through the drawn curtains.

The boy grinned at him. "You sure were out of it."

"I feel like I've been sleeping for days." Tom yawned and realized with relief that he could hear no rain beating at the glass. "Floods drying up?" he asked.

Wes shook his head. "Rained all night."

Tom felt his heart sink. As the rest of him followed suit, slumping back into the mattress, he caught a whiff of how bad his sheets smelled. Small wonder, if he hadn't washed for the best part of a week. Or maybe Marcie had given him sponge baths.

*Gross.*

"You must be bored out of your skull," Wes remarked. "Want to play cards or something?"

Tom raised his bandaged hands and grimaced.

Wes laughed, a little sheepishly. "I guess not. Bummer. I'm bored to *death*."

"Must be tough if you're completely cut off each time it rains," Tom said.

"Yeah," Wes agreed. "And my sister's no fun to hang out with."

"Sister?" Tom suddenly remembered the female voice he'd heard.

"Kate—she's seventeen." Wes said this as if it explained all his problems.

"She hasn't been in to see me," Tom remarked.

Wes looked a little uncomfortable. "Trust me," he said. "You wouldn't want her to right now. She's not in the . . . friendliest of moods."

"Everything okay?" Tom asked.

Wes smiled again. "Sure." Then he shrugged. "Things were different back in Twin Falls."

"Twin Falls, Idaho?"

"Hey, you heard of us!" Wes joked. "I liked it there."

"So why'd you leave?"

"Reasons," said Wes vaguely. "Mom had had it with nursing. And—this was three years ago—Dad's writing was taking off, so . . ."

"Your dad's a writer?" Tom said, impressed.

"Yeah. He's pretty famous. Kids' stuff. I'd tell you his pen name, but then we'd have to kill you." Wes grinned and mimed slitting his throat.

Tom smiled. "So that's why he likes his privacy, I guess. I mean, cutting you all off in this place . . ."

Just then Tom heard a door slam somewhere in the house and a girl's voice bawling someone out. "Kate?" he asked.

Wes looked away. "She just didn't fit in back in Twin Falls, you know? Bad stuff happened. Really bad."

Tom frowned. "Stuff like what?"

Wes shook his head. "You want your nightmares to go away, right?" He got off the bed and walked to the door. "I'd better let you rest up."

"One more thing, Wes," Tom added quickly. "The door." He paused. "Why am I being locked in?"

Wes shifted uncomfortably. "Mom's idea. She doesn't want you sleepwalking. You might get hurt."

"But I feel much better," Tom said. "Really."

"Good," Wes replied, though he looked doubtful as he opened the door. "I'll tell Mom. She'll be pleased to hear that."

Tom watched the door shut behind Wes. But then he heard the quiet, definite click of the key turning.

The door remained locked after each visit. Marcie Folan was adamant that Tom wasn't yet strong enough to roam the house by himself.

*What am I?* Tom wondered uneasily. *An invalid or a prisoner?* He wanted to insist on his freedom, but he felt it would somehow come across as ungrateful. And in any case, he *was* still feeling pretty feeble.

But the locked door bothered him. . . .

Day gradually shriveled into night. The time passed slowly for Tom. For the second time he found himself sinking into that flat, barren nightmare landscape. The deep red sky burned and toughened his skin as he ran in the darkness. But this time something was different. He felt stronger—no longer so afraid. The fierce yellow eyes were no longer fixed on his back, pursuing him. Instead they belonged to the shadowy creature running alongside him, urging him on.

Together the two of them were chasing after something. Something that was running for its life. They would kill it when they caught it, rip into its flesh and—

Tom jerked upright in his bed, wide awake. His heart felt like it was going to burst out of his chest. He forced himself to breathe deeply, wiping away the sweat that drenched his face. He blinked, trying to focus his eyes.

His door was open.

Tom stared at it for a few moments. Then he noticed that a mug of black tea had been left for him on the bedside table. He touched it. Still warm. Whoever had left it had forgotten to lock up again.

This was his chance to see what lay beyond his little room.

Cautiously Tom swung his bandaged legs off the bed and onto the floor. He felt woozy as he tried to stand but managed to hobble over to the door. He winced as he grabbed the door handle—his hands were no longer bandaged but were still swollen and sore. He pulled the door fully open and peered around it to view his surroundings.

Tom was standing at the end of a long corridor painted deep red. He felt strangely light-headed. The polished floorboards were cold under his bare feet as he set off to explore.

Turning the corner, Tom found himself on a landing. A flight of wooden steps to his left spiraled down to a gloomy hallway. To his right was a bathroom, unoccupied, and another door. Light was seeping from its edges.

Maybe this was Wes's room. Tom could hear the murmur of talking downstairs. It sounded like Marcie and Hal. Knowing they weren't nearby gave him the confidence to knock on the door.

No answer.

Almost without thinking, Tom pushed open the door. At least twenty candle flames danced madly in the resultant breeze.

Tom stared around, suddenly uneasy. No way was this Wes's room.

The walls were a deep, dark blue, the color of summer nights. By contrast, the bedspread and wardrobe were dazzling white. A full-length mirror stood in a corner beside a rack of clothes, most of them black. Masks, statues, weird bric-a-brac, and flickering black candles cluttered every surface.

Lying flanked by four scented tea lights was a student ID card. Tom read the name: Mark Fisher. The photo showed a dark-haired boy, about eighteen. The boyfriend, Tom decided. Had to be pretty serious to get the candle treatment. It was like some kind of miniature shrine.

To his right was a small writing desk piled high with old books. He picked up one of them on impulse, sending specks of dust spiraling in the candlelight. The book was so heavy he had to hold it in both hands. The title was stamped into the leather cover in ruddy gold letters:

COVENANTS WITH THE LYCANTHROPE

Tom frowned. *Lycanthrope.* He was sure he knew that word from somewhere.

He opened it up. A bookmark slithered out toward him like a leathery tongue.

The page was filled with old pictures, woodcuts. One showed men dancing with arms outstretched around a large cauldron. Tom read the faded text.

*. . . men would strip to the waist, then rub pungent ointments upon their bodies. Then each would wear a girdle, cut*

*from the pelt of a wolf or the skin of a hanged murderer. Together they would spin and gyrate around the cauldron, inhaling vapors of hemlock, camphor, and extract of belladonna, and call upon evil spirits.*

*They would pray to Satan and the old gods that the wolf inside each man would be released to feed. . . .*

Tom swallowed hard and turned the page. He stared transfixed at chilling pictures, things he could never have imagined. The artist had used only scratchy black ink, but the drawings seemed so real that Tom could almost hear the screams, smell the blood.

He turned the page again. A series of illustrations showed a screaming man being tortured. Tom focused on the description inscribed beneath the pictures.

*Punishment of Peter Stubbe, the first man in Europe accused of being a werewolf, 1632.*

At the bottom of the page were some dull red-brown splotches. Tom's senses twitched. He knew in an instant that they were bloodstains.

Before he could stop himself, he bent his head and touched them with his tongue. The dusty paper stuck to his mouth. Something stirred deep within him.

Convulsing suddenly with horror and disgust, Tom threw the book against the wall. His insides squirmed. What had made him do that?

Suddenly he realized someone was standing in the doorway. A girl. In a black dress.

It could only be Wes's sister, Kate.

She was tall—almost as tall as Tom—with long, dark hair that fell to her slim waist. Her wide green eyes stared at him from a pale, striking face.

Flustered, Tom opened his mouth to speak, but his tongue was burning. He stood there, sweating, silent, and paralyzed.

"What are you doing?" she asked sharply. "This is my room."

"Kate?" Tom began. "I'm sorry. . . ."

"Get out of here," she hissed. The candle flames danced again as she swept past Tom into the room. "Go on, leave."

Tom felt the room spin around him. Wes was right. He should've stayed put in bed. Safe in his little cell. "I didn't know it was your room," he said groggily, holding up his chapped and swollen hands in apology.

"I see your hands haven't healed," she said, her voice a little softer, sadder.

Tom stared dumbly at his fingers. "The riverbank . . . deadly nightshade."

"Deadly . . ." Kate's short, high laugh was humorless. "Whatever else you are, you're no Boy Scout, are you?"

"Huh?" Tom frowned.

"Deadly nightshade—belladonna," Kate elaborated. "You won't have seen it anywhere near the riverbank. In fact, you won't see it growing anywhere in the state."

What was she talking about? Her angular features kept blurring in and out of focus. "So, the belladonna on my hands . . ." Tom murmured. "How . . . ?"

Was Kate shaking, or was that just his vision swimming again?

"Cultivated. Here," she said quietly. "Get out of this house. While you still can."

Tom could hear approaching footsteps. And in the same moment he realized Kate wasn't angry or frightened by him. She was frightened *for* him.

The footfalls drew closer, then two dark shapes loomed in the doorway.

"Tom?"

Groggy as Tom was, there was no mistaking Marcie Folan's matronly tones.

"You should be in bed, Tom."

Tom heard Hal's deeper voice say quietly, "I thought we were keeping his door locked?"

"Must've been Wesley," Marcie muttered back. "You know what the boy's like. No sense."

Kate had fallen silent now.

Tom's eyes closed. He felt his legs buckle; then a pair of strong arms caught him and carried him out of Kate's bedroom along the landing back toward his own.

The next thing Tom knew he was back in bed, shivering with cold even while his body felt like it was burning up. "Kate," he said indistinctly. "Her books . . . the pictures . . ."

He heard Marcie laugh, a thin, reedy sound. "You're not scared of those old things, are you, Tom?"

"Maybe he's scared of Kate." Though Hal was almost hidden in the shadows at the foot of the bed, there was no hiding the smile in his voice.

"That's not true, now, is it?" Marcie seemed to be telling Tom more than asking him. She held a glass of water to his lips, and he obediently sipped. It tasted strangely sweet. "Kate and you have a lot in common. You'll see. You're going to get along great."

As they left the room, Tom was already slipping away, back into the dark place.

He just about heard the lightning-quick turn of the key in the lock. And then he was falling straight back into his nightmare. . . .

He was running again, over that black and featureless plain—but this time on all fours. The yellow-eyed shadow beast was there again beside him, setting the pace. Sweat prickled his aching body as he bounded along faster and faster, unable to stop.

He woke suddenly, heart pounding, bones aching like he'd been running for real. For a few confused moments, to be chasing like that, to feel that power and strength, had seemed like the most natural thing in the world.

## CHAPTER FOUR

Two more days crawled by, slowly and sweatily. Now that Tom was feeling a little better, time hung more heavily about him. Like the thick, smothering blankets he always kicked off in his fitful sleep.

He decided it was time to assert himself.

"I need to get back to the mainland," he announced to Marcie when she came to bring him soup one evening. "My family will be *totally* freaking by now."

"Uh-uh," she said with a sad shake of the head. "Sorry, honey. The causeway is still flooded. No way out."

"But the police could get through, couldn't they?" Tom screwed up his nose as Marcie placed the soup on the table. It smelt of cumin and ginger, almost overpoweringly so. "Or an air ambulance. They could bring Mom and Dad here. You know, just to see that I'm okay."

"They could if we could get a message to them," Marcie agreed. "But we can't, remember?"

Tom couldn't believe it. "But what if you ever had a real emergency here?"

Hal stepped into the room, grave faced. "We look out for ourselves pretty well, Tom. We keep strangers away. If people round here realized who I was, I'd never know a minute's peace."

Tom slumped back into his heavy pillows. "I . . . I appreciate that, Mr. Folan, and I'm grateful for everything you guys have done, but—"

"Just drink your soup and relax, Tom," Marcie soothed. "I think the causeway should be safe to cross by tomorrow afternoon. And if it is, we'll drive you straight back to your folks. Okay?"

Tom stared at her, almost afraid to believe her. "You mean it?"

Marcie looked him straight in the eyes. "Would I say it if I didn't mean it?"

"Now drink your soup," said Hal. He smiled reassuringly before ducking back out of the room.

"Thanks," Tom told Marcie, hugely relieved. He began to eat. The taste was incredible. Tom found he could pick out the exact flavor of every vegetable, every herb. His head was buzzing, heart pounding at the thought of seeing his family again.

As Marcie turned to leave, Tom quickly called out to her. "So, I guess I don't need the door locked anymore, right?"

"Right," she agreed. "In fact, I thought you might

like to come join us downstairs later. Kate's anxious to say sorry about the other night."

Tom put down his empty bowl, his mood suddenly more wary. "Not a problem," he muttered.

Marcie nodded. "I'll call you when dinner's ready," she said with a smile, leaving the door wide open behind her.

Tom was left staring at a plain slab of the passage wall. Dark crimson. The color of congealed blood.

He thought of Kate and a shiver went through him. *"She just didn't fit in back in Twin Falls, you know?"* Wesley had told him. *"Bad stuff happened. Really bad."*

A part of him wanted to get out of bed and pull the door tightly shut again. "I've been stuck here too long," he muttered to himself. "I'm going crazy. Tomorrow I'll be out of here. Everything's going to be fine."

Bored and restless, looking away from the open door, he found himself listening to the clatter of pans in the kitchen downstairs. Sound sure did carry in this house. He could even hear the sizzling of oil in a skillet around raw meat. Burgers. The smell was almost overpowering. His mouth began to water, so fast he could barely swallow the saliva down. He hadn't realized just what the heavy oak door had been shutting out all this time.

He scrambled out of bed, fighting against a wave of dizziness. The meat sizzling seemed to fill his ears. Its aroma was hitting the back of his head like smelling salts. It was like his senses had been suddenly sharpened and now the world was too loud, too bright, a mass of skin-crawling sensations.

He collapsed to the floor, hands over his ears, feeling like he was going to throw up.

A scuttling noise sounded close by, and he felt a trembling through the threadbare carpet: the light skittering of bugs and other creatures in the dark beneath the floorboards.

*You're imagining it,* he told himself. *All of it.* But he could barely hear the voice in his head for the din all about him.

Shivering, he crawled back into bed, willing the too-loud, too-bright world to go away and leave him in quiet shadows again.

He had to get out of this place tomorrow. Before it drove him totally out of his mind.

The next thing Tom knew, someone was calling him from downstairs. Marcie.

He checked the bedside clock. He'd been asleep for a couple of hours, and things felt more normal, quieter. His head ached, and there was a vile taste in his mouth, but at least he wasn't hallucinating now.

"Hey, Tom!" That was Wesley's voice. It sounded almost mocking. "You coming down for a bite?"

"Sure," Tom called out hoarsely. He lurched out of bed and stumbled over to the open door. "Two minutes."

He noticed something at his feet. A pile of clean clothes. Wesley's, he guessed. He pulled them on.

It felt weird to be dressed again but good, too. Healthier. Like convalescence was coming to an end at last. Tom looked at himself in the cracked mirror above the dresser, smoothed back his dark bangs. His cheeks were hollow and patchily stubbled; he had more beard than he'd expected for having gone only a few days without shaving. The shirt was a bit baggy, but it looked better than the rumpled T-shirt he'd pretty much lived in since he wound up here.

Something was in his pants pocket. A roll of mints—nice touch.

As he padded out along the corridor, he saw that the light was off in Kate's room.

Nervous, he walked down the stairs into the spacious living room. The walls were bare and bleached like the uncarpeted floorboards. Flames crackled over a cluster of coals in a massive granite fireplace but seemed to spread no warmth. The high ceiling was crisscrossed with exposed beams, the worn wood the same dark hue as the teetering bookcases and well-polished occasional tables below.

At first Tom wondered if his head's volume control was acting up again, only this time turned way too low instead of cranked up really high. But no. The heavy silence in the room was real, and it made Tom wish he could go straight back to bed.

"Good to see you up." Marcie smiled at Tom expectantly.

"I feel much better," said Tom uneasily. He tried to catch Wesley's eye, but he was slumped in a chair, thumbs working over a handheld computer game, staring at the little screen like no one else existed. As for Hal, he was nowhere to be seen. Then Tom realized Marcie was gesturing across at a swivel chair with its back turned to him.

"Kate, darling," she said. "Tom's here. I *know* you want to talk to him."

Tom heard a soft sigh as the chair swiveled slowly around. Then he began to blush. Kate was dressed for a date. Her long dark hair was piled up on her head, and she was wearing a deep green low-cut dress that looked like it was silk or something. A string of jade beads hung elegantly around her porcelain neck, each one as cold and pale as her narrowed eyes.

"Hi," she said.

Tom's face felt like it was burning. "I'm, uh . . . I'm sorry we got off to a bad start. You know, me coming into your room and all."

"Forget it," said Kate dismissively. She got up and crossed to one of the couches.

Tom could feel Marcie's eyes flicking between the pair of them.

"Why don't you sit beside Kate, Tom?" she said.

"He's got sense, that's why," murmured Wesley.

"That's enough out of you," hissed Marcie.

Tom recoiled from the venom in her voice, even though it wasn't directed at him.

Wesley gave a pantomime shrug. "Later," he called over his shoulder in Tom's direction. He slunk away, pale and edgy.

Hal passed Wes coming out of the kitchen. He was holding a tray of party food—slices of quiche, pigs in blankets and stuff. This was getting majorly weird.

Tom perched on the couch beside Kate. She wriggled away a couple of inches. Hal set down the tray in front of them. Tom thanked him, though the hot, pungent smell of sausage turned his guts. He sucked the last of his mint as discreetly as possible.

The silence was excruciating. Time to try again. "You look, uh, good, Kate. All dressed up and nowhere to go, huh?"

"I haven't been let out for days," Kate said sullenly.

Tom frowned. "How could you go out? The causeway's blocked, right?"

Kate looked at her mother. "Whoops. I keep coming out with them, don't I?"

"Figure of speech," Marcie put in smoothly.

"Eat something." Hal spoke softly, but the words sounded more like an order than a suggestion.

Tom took a slice of the quiche, but the stink of Gruyere cheese was way too strong. He grimaced.

"Homemade," Marcie said encouragingly. "Kate's quite the chef."

"My stomach's still a little upset," Tom murmured, putting the slice down.

Kate looked away, making a scoffing sound at the back of her throat like she didn't believe him.

Just for a moment Tom caught her scent, musky but with a sweet, mossy smell like raspberries about it. It was so good, it all but wiped out his other senses.

In a daze, he realized he was sitting there looking at her like some kind of freak.

"What are you staring at?" she inquired acidly.

"He's staring because you look beautiful tonight," suggested Hal. "Doesn't she, Tom?"

"Uh, yeah." This was *so* weird. Tom wished the ground would open and swallow him up, no matter how many bugs were scuttling around down there. "Yeah, she does."

Kate stood up. Tom saw she was trembling as she turned to her mother. "This is sick. Pathetic. Just what the hell are you expecting?"

"Some manners, sweetie?" Marcie's voice was like ice cracking.

"I think maybe I should go back to bed," Tom announced too loudly, feeling almost light-headed. "Better rest up if I'm leaving tomorrow. . . ."

Kate looked like she was about to say something but changed her mind. "Good night, then," she said.

Tom nodded, smiled awkwardly, and moved

toward the stairs. What the hell had all *that* been about?

"Wait down here, Kate," said Hal. "We need to have a little talk, don't you think?"

"You *all* need to have a little talk," muttered Tom to himself as he walked up the stairs, "with a shrink." All the same, a part of him wished he could hear what was going to be said next.

As he reached the top of the stairs, he found he could.

Even as he moved farther along the landing, by concentrating on the low voices downstairs he could still make out every word. Weird, but it kind of figured. The acoustics in this house were as crazy as the people who lived in it.

"You need to warm up your attitude, you icy little bitch."

That was Marcie. Tom blinked in surprise. Nice pep talk.

"Remember Mark?" Hal added. "Don't let that happen again, sweetheart. Please."

Mark. The boyfriend. Then with a shiver Tom remembered the candles burning for him in Kate's room.

"Poor, sweet Mark," agreed Marcie. "He liked you so much. And when you wouldn't play ball, well . . . it just tore him apart." Her voice hardened. "Remember?"

"You disgust me."

Tom could hear the quaver in Kate's voice as she tried to hold back tears.

"Not as much as you disgust me," replied Marcie coldly. "You're soft. Toothless. A frightened rabbit when you could be . . . so much more."

Tom strained to hear now over the thudding of his heart. To hear a mother say that stuff to her own child . . . He thought of his own parents, closed his eyes, and wished they were here now.

Marcie's voice had fallen to a hoarse whisper. "But none of that matters. This is going to happen, just as you promised it would. There's no way out for you. None."

Tom listened on in a kind of trance.

"Dad?" Kate sounded like a little girl now, pleading for help.

"Accept it, Kate," he said softly. "It's for your own good. For the good of the family."

"Well, I *hate* this family," Kate hissed. Then she was thundering up the stairs. Angry. Defiant. *"All of you!"*

Whoa. Tom ducked inside his room and quietly shut the door, terrified without really knowing why. Kate's muffled sobs from the bathroom sounded down the landing.

He stood there listening to them for some time.

Kate turned off the bath faucets. The bathroom was filled with steam. The water pipes hissed like a nest of vipers.

She dipped her foot in the scalding water, felt the heat bite into her skin. With a soft whimper she plunged in first one leg, then the other, and stood there in the overflowing tub, trembling.

She bit her lip, screwed up her eyes. The hairs on her arms were standing up with the shock of it. Slowly, soundlessly she crouched, sank through the acid burn of the steaming water's surface. Finally a choked gasp escaped her.

The pain was excruciating, the water like fire.

Purifying fire.

She needed to feel clean.

"Remember Mark," her father had said.

Like she could ever, ever forget.

His pale face. Blue eyes wide and fearful. Clammy hands grasping for hers.

Kate wished she could dissolve in the searing water. She couldn't keep the scene from replaying in her mind. . . .

*"I love you, Kate," Mark says, just the way he always does, ever since a few days after they met. But his eyes are slightly glazed now, his skin beaded with sweat, like he's taken something.*

*Kate sees the ugly wound in his neck, the bruised and puckered skin around it, and feels tears building. "I told you never to come here. I told you. . . ."*

*"Couldn't keep away." He smiles goofily.*

*"We said we'd wait! Wait till I finished school, till I—"*

*"Oh, baby, all that time apart . . . You know I'm smitten."*

*He giggles suddenly. "Smitten and bitten now . . . Just think what we'll be able to do together. . . ."*

*Kate can't believe what she's hearing. "So now you know what my family is—and you're okay with it? You actually want this?"*

*Mark glances behind to where Marcie stands, watching. Then he turns back to Kate and nods. "I'm glad," he drawls. "C'mon, Kate. Say you'll do it. For me—for us . . ." He tries to pull her to him.*

*Kate shrugs him away, her heart breaking. She can't let him touch her. "You don't know what you're saying."*

*She turns to Marcie. "I'll never forgive you for this."*

*Marcie smiles coldly. "Blessed be the bite. It's a natural high, sweetheart. If the spirit is willing . . ."*

*Mark clumsily reaches for Kate again. "I'm still your Mark, baby . . ." he protests.*

*"No!" Kate shakes her head fiercely. "No, you're not. You're one of them now."*

*Mark turns to Marcie. "She'll come around in time. We love each other."*

*Kate feels a knife twist in her guts. She dashes away her tears, then turns to her mother. "No way am I playing this sick game of yours. Not now, not ever. I'm not going to let you rule my life!"*

*A tight-lipped smile appears on Marcie's face. "Is that a fact? What a shame. I thought if I turned someone you cared about, you'd be grateful. It's more choice than I ever got."*

*"I'm not sacrificing myself for your sick dream!"*

*Marcie shakes her head. "You're not going to change*

*your mind, are you, Kate? All you care about is yourself."*
*She looks at Mark. "Sorry, honey. I really hoped this would work out. But I guess she just doesn't think you're The One after all."*

*Kate, feeling the slow burn of betrayal, shrinks from them both in disgust. Then her breath catches in her throat as Marcie suddenly drops to all fours.*

*Marcie licks her lips. "But hey, Mark, do you know what I think you are? Dinner."*

*"No!' Kate shrieks. "You wouldn't—"*

*The change comes easily to Marcie. A thick stream of drool floods from her mouth as she readies herself to jump. "I think your girlfriend needs a lesson," she snarls, arching her back. "She does things my way—or not at all."*

*Mark stands there, frozen in shock.*

*Kate runs for him to give him whatever protection her slim body will allow.*

*Too late.*

Kate sat straight up in the steaming bath. The tears poured down her face. She splashed the stinging water against her cheeks, rubbed it into her eyes.

It was no good. She would never be clean.

She rose unsteadily and got out of the tub.

She'd sworn then that no one else would die because of her, that she'd go along with whatever Marcie wanted. But she knew with a sick certainty, deep down, that when it came to it, she would never be able to give herself. And that by kidding herself all this time that she could play along, she'd doomed Tom Anderson. He would go the same way as Mark. And what would she do then?

She toweled her burning body dry, slipped on a robe, and went to her room. The tea-light candles burning round Mark's ID card had gone out.

*I have to stop what's happening,* she realized wearily. *I have to save Tom. Before it's too late.*

## CHAPTER FIVE

Tom was feeling more alive than he'd ever imagined possible. His heightened senses earlier that evening hadn't been a hallucination. They were back, crowding through his head. And he was learning to control them: if he stopped and concentrated, the mundane workings of the world about him became so intense he could barely stand it. If his mind wandered, his voracious senses slunk back into sleep, and everything seemed normal.

As normal as it could get in this house.

Like thirty minutes ago. He'd heard Kate's door opening and her quiet footsteps coming out into the hallway. Then . . .

"What's in the folder?" Marcie had asked. She must have been passing Kate's door at the time.

Kate had been irritated, defensive. "It's nothing. Puzzles and stuff. I thought he might be bored. I'm just trying to make the effort, like you *want* me to."

"That's sweet, but you heard the boy," Marcie

said softly. "He wants to rest up. And I think you've said enough to him today, don't you?"

"Forget it." Kate had gone back inside her room and slammed the door.

"You're not to go to his room," Marcie hissed. "I'll be watching."

Nuts. Everyone here was nuts. He heard Hal and Wes arguing now. Wes wanted to go out in the woods.

"For the last time, no one is going out tonight!" Hal yelled. "There's meat in the freezer. We don't know when the boy's going to . . ."

The words were suddenly lost in the lo-fi thud and blare of some hard-core hip-hop. Tom smiled grudgingly. Nicely played, Wes. If you can't leave the house, make it tough on everyone else stuck inside.

Tom reached a decision. With the blaring music covering his tracks, he could take a look around. Maybe talk to Kate, ask her what the hell was going on here. Or at least apologize for being such an utter doofus downstairs.

He crept stealthily along the corridor—then froze as he heard footsteps descending the stairs. Marcie. She must have meant it about watching Kate. So why give up now? A second later the sound of the shower gurgling into life gave him his answer; Tom doubted that a soaking wet Kate was about to come running into his room with a soggy pile of puzzles.

He turned the corner. Kate's bedroom door was ajar, so he stepped inside.

His eyes adjusted surprisingly quickly to the dim candlelight. A red folder sat by the pillow. He opened it up and found it stuffed with newspaper clippings. Even a cursory glance gave him the gist of it: a spate of missing persons and violent murders in Twin Falls, Idaho. The last one was dated three years ago. About the time the family moved away, Wes had told him.

He suddenly got the creepy feeling he was being watched. But when he turned around, the only eyes on him were those of Mystery Mark looking out sightlessly from his student card through the flames of fresh candles.

Tom closed the folder, a chill shivering down his spine. As he did so, he noticed a note scrawled on a yellow sticky on the back of the file.

*Pull back the sheet*
*Get rid of it*

With an uneasy feeling he pushed Kate's pillow and quilt to one side, then paused. Did he really want to do this? He could smell traces of her scent on the bedding. Such a good smell . . .

Tom's face grew hot with embarrassment. Great. He was sniffing around girls' bedrooms. Maybe he should go through her underwear next.

Holding his breath, with a sharp yank Tom tugged a corner of the pristine white sheet away.

Nothing was there. Just a pink-patterned mattress.

Tom put things back just as he'd found them and left the room. But as he arrived back at his own, there was the quiet crack of a pebble at the window.

Tom sat up, senses alert again.

Something hit the wall below the window with a thud.

He leapt out of bed and crossed to see what was going on.

Beyond the jutting lip of the porch roof beneath him, Tom caught a fleeting glimpse of Kate, ducking from sight. But the shower was still running! How had she gotten out there? He opened the window and craned his neck around to see if he could catch sight of her again.

What he saw instead was the towering spire of what must have been a ham radio antenna. The mast bisected the full moon, beaming down at him from a starless sky. In that bright glare he noticed too what seemed to be a telephone cable snaking across the brickwork above his window.

At once he broke out in a cold sweat, felt suddenly breathless. He willed himself to stay calm. Okay, so they had a ham radio and a phone line. They could have gotten a message out to the authorities about him if they'd wanted to. But maybe it was broken. And the phone line might be an old one, disconnected when they came here . . .

Or maybe not.

He couldn't concentrate with the moon shining so

brightly in his eyes. It was like staring into a hundred-watt bulb. His skin was tingling like he had a sunburn, and a surge of panic and nausea welled up inside him.

He hung out through the window in case he was sick. And he saw what had thudded onto the porch roof. Tentatively he reached for it.

A newspaper, wrapped around a rock and held there with a rubber band.

Why was Kate throwing old newspapers at him? No one had gone out to pick up a new one. No one *could* get out. . . .

He stared at the date. Blinked. Stared again. This had to be a joke. A misprint.

The newspaper was dated September 16. He'd gone swimming, been faced down by a bear, smashed himself stupid on August 17. And that had been just a week ago. Right?

The world seemed to tilt away from him.

Tom staggered back away from the window and collapsed with the paper on the bed. He tore through its oversized pages, scanning the print for anything familiar in the news, stuff that would show up the mistake with the date.

His eyes froze on a small headline circled in red ink. The column was buried right in the middle near the classifieds. The sort of page where old news goes to die.

HOPES FADE FOR MISSING BOY

His eyes flicked over the story, his mind numbly cataloging the bones of it. "Youth missing for a month . . . Clothes found by riverbank . . . bear tracks . . . no sign of a body . . . family advised to prepare for the worst . . ."

Then he took in the missing boy's name.

". . . Sixteen-year-old Tom Anderson . . ."

He stared, transfixed. Tears welled up from some cold place deep inside.

Everything he'd been told was a lie.

The Folans could contact the outside world anytime they chose. They just chose not to.

They'd chosen to keep him here for almost a month while feeding him crap about the flooded causeway—crap he'd swallowed like a good little invalid. And that was another thing. For them to fool him about the time like that . . . he must have been drugged.

*"My herbal cures have been fixing you up,"* Marcie had said. *"Better than any drugs a hospital can give you."*

He looked at his still-swollen hands. He'd come into contact with belladonna, Marcie had said. Then Kate had told him belladonna was cultivated here. So why . . . ?

He bit his lip. Started to shake.

*Nah. Get real. Couldn't be.*

In that old book of Kate's it said belladonna formed part of the ritual that made men into werewolves. What else—hemlock? Camphor? Those

51

ointments Marcie had been rubbing into his skin . . .

The image of the yellow sticky note flashed into his brain.

*Pull back the sheet*

*Get rid of it*

There'd been nothing on Kate's bed. Because she'd meant to bring the folder to *his* room. The message was for *him*. It was *his* sheet she was talking about.

Slowly, carefully, Tom eased himself off the bed like it might devour him if he made any sudden moves. He pushed aside the pillow and quilt, then pulled out one corner of the sheet from beneath the mattress.

As he yanked the sheet away, he saw it.

He backed away, wanted to cry out in horror, but the bile was too hot and sharp in his throat.

There, stretched across the mattress like some well-fed, basking animal, was the thick, sleek pelt of a wolf.

# CHAPTER SIX

Kate sneaked carefully back into the house, shutting the kitchen door soundlessly behind her. It was a routine she was well used to. You could get *out* through the bathroom window if you were ready to risk the drop down into the bushes, but you couldn't get back in the same way. Wesley used the route regularly—he had to, seeing as he'd been grounded for most of his teens—but Kate hadn't sneaked out the window way. She had no one to see, nowhere to go.

She could hear the hissing of the hot-water pipes in the wall beside her. Had her ruse with the shower been enough to convince her mother to give up guard duty for twenty minutes?

Beside her, on the wooden countertop, was a huge hunk of raw meat. Deer, probably; there used to be a lot in the forest. Blood pooled stickily around it and was dripping down onto the usually spotless floor.

Kate looked away, revolted, and saw another

hunk of meat lying in the corner by the washing machine. Judging by the messy track marks, she thought it had been kicked there. Mom must be having one of her "moods."

Kate took a deep breath. When Marcie was like this . . .

Over the muffled beats of Wesley's music she could hear her mother flipping out at Hal in the living room. Guard duty looked like it was no longer Marcie's priority. Her tone was charged with the hopeless urgency of a crazy person.

There was no way Kate could sneak past them to get to the stairs.

"But I *need* to go out and kill," said Marcie, like this was the most reasonable thing in the world. "Come on, honey. *Please,* baby. I want it. That's only natural, isn't it? You must want it too. . . . Let's just go *do* it."

Kate's father responded uneasily, talking to Marcie like she was a child: "Marcie, we agreed we'd cut back on the—"

"Don't give me that 'we agreed' crap!" Marcie shrieked. "It's what *you* agreed, you son of a bitch!"

Kate tiptoed to the kitchen door. She opened it a fraction.

"Marcie, the boy must be close to turning," Hal said reasonably. "We need to be here for him when—"

"Hal, baby, be here for *me* right now, okay? *Please.* I need to go out." Marcie was quieter now.

Her slow, sly voice was somehow scarier than the yelling. "I'm not strong and stoic like you. I can't live off cold, dead stuff my whole life."

"You go feeding too much. Stray too far."

Marcie growled, a guttural rumbling. "I can't stop."

"You can. We all can. It's a *choice;* we don't have to—" Hal broke off.

Hal had seen Kate. But she didn't care if he knew she'd been out. Defiance flared inside her. "So it *is* a choice!' she spat at him.

Hal didn't react, just stared at her. Then he turned back to his wife, keeping her attention on him. "Please. Stay in with me."

"What part of this aren't you getting, Hal?" Marcie sighed. She cupped his face. With each whispered word a different nail gouged the skin on his cheek: "I'm—going—outside—tonight."

Kate watched as her father put his fingertips to his scratched face and took them away, slick with blood. Her mother kissed his cheek, rubbed her face against it.

Hal looked over at Kate. "Go on," he mouthed to her.

Kate nodded and crossed the room silently to the stairs.

Marcie was clinging to Hal now like she was too drunk to stand. She laughed, a harsh rattling sound. "I'll bring you back something real nice, Hal. Nice romantic dinner for two, right?"

As Kate quickly climbed the stairs, she couldn't help looking back at the thing that was her mother snuffling at her father's bleeding face. His eyes met hers for a moment.

Each could see the fear in the other's.

Tom stared at the pelt stretched tight across the bed for what seemed like forever. Then he tore it free with jerky movements and rolled it up as tightly as he could. It felt warm from his lying on it and smelled of aniseed and smoke.

And of him.

He slung the pelt to the corner of his room with all the strength he could muster. Then he buried it completely beneath bedclothes.

He was hyperventilating. *Fresh air.* He needed fresh air. He staggered over to the window—then recoiled from the bright, bloated moon shining through the glass. Sweeping the curtains closed, Tom sank back against the wall.

Just what had the Folans done to him? Something was wrong with him, horribly wrong. All the weird stuff he'd been going through, it had seemed so random at first. But now it was starting to add up. And the answer seemed crazy. . . .

The violent dreams of a hunched creature with yellow eyes . . . the old books and belladonna . . . the way his senses had sharpened . . . the moon tugging him to the window . . . the pelt on the bed . . .

Mystical, superstitious crap. Stuff to scare little kids with.

Except it was really happening.

He wasn't sure how much time passed before the front door slammed shut downstairs, making him jump. A few moments later Wesley's music was switched off.

Tom's skin was squirming like there were bugs beneath it, driving him out of his mind. He needed some proper answers.

Kate. Surely she would help him?

He stretched out with his senses, realized the shower had stopped running. Kate must've gotten back inside the house undetected or he'd have heard the fuss—right? He stumbled out of his room and down the corridor to the landing and raised his fist to knock on her door.

"Hey, Tom."

He spun around. Wesley was perched halfway up the stairs. In the glare of the landing light his red hair seemed brighter than ever, emphasizing his pale complexion. He looked sick and sweaty, but there was the ghost of a smile on his face as he looked up at Tom, gray eyes gleaming. "So . . . want to hang out?"

Tom stared down at him. The words came boiling out. "What have you done to me?"

Wesley's smile grew broader.

"You all . . . You said I'd been here a week." Tom gritted his teeth. "It's been a month."

Wesley snickered. "Well, time flies when you're having fun." He turned and walked down the stairs.

"Wait." Tom started after him, almost losing his balance. His head was buzzing, the itch inside him growing, but he kept going down the stairs. He had to stay angry. Anger would give him a focus. "I'm not through with you, Wesley," he snarled.

At this, Wesley turned around, eyebrows raised, amused. "Is that right?"

Tom took a step closer. "What have you done to me?"

"You're the big tough guy now, right?" Wesley shook his head. "I think you know what we've done to you."

"I think you and your whole family are crazy . . . delusional. You all get off on thinking you're something you're not, and for some sick reason you've kidnapped me to make me think I'm like that too."

"Like *what,* Tom?" Wesley cupped a hand to his ear, making out he was deaf. "I want to hear you say the word."

"You think you're . . ." Tom flushed. "You think you're wolf people or something."

"Wolf people?" Wesley spluttered with laughter, then slicked back his hair with both hands. "I think the term you're looking for is *werewolves?*"

"You think this is funny?" Tom snapped. He marched up to Wesley and shoved him with both hands, knocking him to the floor. "Think it's some big joke?"

"Hey, I'm just happy for you, man," said Wesley, getting up. "You're one of us now. You were a tough turn, but we got you." He smirked, and a flash of yellow seemed to glow through his eyes. "Welcome to the family."

"What the hell are you talking about?" Tom demanded.

Wesley pointed to his shoulder. "You were *bitten,* man. On the riverbank."

Tom closed his eyes, remembering. *Two narrowed yellow eyes, glinting, low down in the shadows.* "But it was barely dark then," he argued desperately. "Werewolves only change at night, under a full moon."

"Sure, Tom." Wesley's voice dripped with sarcasm. "And guess what? There really *is* a Santa Claus." He laughed. "Night helps, true. But if you're sharp, you can bring on the change whenever."

Tom tried to shake his throbbing head like he didn't believe it. "You really believe this crap, don't you?"

Wesley ignored him. "We mostly bite to kill. For the buzz, you know? But Mom had her eye on you for Kate from the minute she saw you in the woods, playing happy camper with your folks." He laughed. "Dad made me go with her. He didn't trust her not to eat you all up instead of just giving you the bite."

Tom screwed up his eyes. *This isn't real, isn't real.*

"As it turned out, you put up a fight. A regular silverblood."

"Silverblood?" Tom echoed.

"You wouldn't turn. Wouldn't give in to the infection. Your body kept resisting. We had to work you over with Mom's potions and shit, keep you here till the moon was full again. And now . . ." Wesley smirked again. "Gotcha."

Tom took a step back. "You've lost it, Wesley," he said, wishing he could really believe it. "You've lost it, big time."

Wesley shook his head. "Uh-uh . . . *You've* lost it—half your human side," he said softly, gray eyes gleaming. "You're lupine now. Half wolf."

"No. This isn't real." Tom stared around wildly, half hoping for hidden cameras to come into the open, for some smart-ass TV host to appear from nowhere and have a good laugh at his expense. "This is crap, all of it."

"No," snapped Wesley. He wasn't laughing now as he threw himself at Tom, grabbed hold of his neck, and tried to wrestle him to the floorboards. "No, it's not. What's your problem? We don't make a habit of bestowing a wolf side to soft meat—it's an honor!"

Tom tried to fight him off. "Screw your honor. Screw you!"

But Wesley pinned Tom's arms behind his head with one hand, kept his grip on Tom's neck with the other, and leaned in close. "Wave bye-bye to your old life, Tom," he said softly. "You've lost a family but gained a pack. See, Mom's decided you're the one for Kate. That little snack party earlier?" Wesley squeezed Tom by the throat. "That was matchmaking."

"What? Why?" Tom gasped, lying still, conserving his strength.

"Kate's pureblood female." Wesley shrugged, like this explained everything. "She won't turn 'wolf till she mates with a 'wolf. And for the sake of the Folan family name, Mom wants her to be one of us—*very* badly."

Tom bucked his body as if a thousand volts had been put through him. Twisting at the same time, he managed to throw Wesley clear. Then he got to his feet and backed away toward the kitchen. "I want no part of this," he said hoarsely.

"No way out," sneered Wesley, climbing to his feet. "You've been *chosen*. Hell, even Kate finally said yes. To save you from winding up like poor sweet Mark."

Tom rubbed his bruised neck. "You killed him?"

"Mom did." Wesley licked his lips. "He was a real spurter."

"Murderers," Tom breathed.

"You'll understand. When the change comes."

"It's never going to come." But Tom's fingers rasped against inflamed skin near his collarbone.

The bite mark. It itched now like someone had sewn up a live moth inside it.

"Come on, Tom." Wesley's voice was friendly, reasonable. "You've thrown your fit. Now let's quit fooling around and start to party."

Tom turned to the window and felt the moonlight on his skin. It wasn't burning him now. It was soothing him. Taking away the confusion, the questions, even the pain. All he felt now was his loss and his anger, cold and clear as the dead reflected light from the moon's barren surface.

"Face it, Tom," Wes whispered. "You're in this for keeps. Kate's going to marry you so Mom can have some 'wolf grandkids to keep up our family line. She needs them, see? The time's coming when werewolves won't need to hide in the shadows."

Tom stared in horror. "There are more of you?"

"Thousands of us," Wesley said. "All over the world. When Wolf Time comes, it'll be humans hiding out in the dark, not us. That's when the Old Names are going to count, see? When it comes to thrashing out the biting order in our new world." Flecks of white saliva began to collect at the corners of Wesley's mouth. "You're lucky I bit you, Tom. Now you've got a big stake in this family. Come Wolf Time, you and me are going to rule the rest."

"*You* did this to me," Tom whispered.

"What are friends for?" Wesley grinned mockingly. "Now how about we go on the hunt, huh?"

Tom stared down at his feet. He could feel his heart start to pound. "Hunt?"

"Sure. We're supposed to stay in, but screw that. Mom and Dad are out on the hunt; they'll be gone till sunrise. So what say we—?"

Tom lashed out. His fist smashed into Wesley's jaw, sending him sprawling over the kitchen table.

"So you want to play it this way, huh?" Wesley growled.

"Turn me back." Tom's voice was hoarse.

"No can do." Wesley wiped blood from his mouth and sucked it back off his knuckles.

"Turn me back!" Tom yelled. He hefted a vase from the fireplace and threw it at Wesley's head.

Wesley jumped aside and the vase shattered on the floorboards beside him. "It's started," he said in a hushed voice. He looked at Tom almost reverently, like he was seeing a baby take its first steps. "Man, I envy you, feeling it all for the first time."

"Shut up!" Tom shouted. His breathing was getting ragged; his clothes were drenched with sweat.

Wesley was nodding, suddenly totally focused, like he was Tom's personal trainer or something. "That's it. Keep your anger; that helps push it on." He paused, smiling craftily. "Y'know, just to make things final, maybe we should go kill your family."

Tom felt like he was burning. "I'm warning you. . . ."

"Yeah, it'd be easy," Wesley mused. "Once we offed your parents, we could, like, string up your brother and take turns biting chunks out of him."

A red haze swam in front of Tom's eyes. As Wesley laughed, Tom rushed for him wildly. But Wesley sidestepped him and punched him in the stomach. Tom doubled over, winded, then gasped as Wesley twisted his arm behind his back.

The moon burned like a spotlight through the window. Its glow seemed to follow Tom as Wesley threw him across the room, lighting every move.

"What's the matter?" Wesley crooned. He kicked Tom in the head. "Gonna cry? Don't go soft on me. Come on! I want to see it happen!" He kicked him again.

Tom's body smashed against the display case, and its glass front cracked in two under the impact. Tom saw duplicate moons reflected there, white eyes staring out at him. He tried to speak, but only guttural grunts came. His body twisted in pain. He couldn't breathe. Vivid colors broke across his vision.

*"Come on!"* screamed Wesley.

Tom felt like every bone in his body was starting to crack and splinter, like some invisible vise was crushing them from the inside.

Then something broke inside his head, and the pain fell away, replaced with a warm, reckless ecstasy. A part of him knew instinctively that it was wrong to feel this way. That feeling so good could only come with some terrible price attached.

It was like all his life he'd been peering out at the

world through dirty glass and only now could he see it clearly—be fully a part of it. Sounds and scents sharpened and spun dizzily through his senses. Every nerve in his body seemed to buzz with a life of its own. He heard a strange sound, half laughing, half roaring. Then he realized he was making the noise himself.

Wesley had fallen away. Tom rose to his knees and saw his opponent slumped in a corner, shaking like he was having some kind of fit. Tom tried to stand up, to see more, but his body didn't want to turn that way.

It wanted to stay on all fours.

Tom stared as a hideous creature, half man, half wolf, kicked itself free from the remains of Wesley's clothing. And then some dwindling, terrified part of Tom truly took the situation in.

*"You think you're wolf people or something,"* he had said. At the time he'd truly believed the Folans were just deluded—a family of psychos hiding deep in the woods.

But not now. The werewolf staring him down from across the room, yellow eyes flaring with malice, sinewy body tensed to attack, was no mythical beast.

Wesley Folan was a werewolf.

And Tom was one, too.

The old Tom Anderson was dead, washed away by the rapids all those weeks ago to some lonely burial far out at sea. A new creature that wore his skin had crept in to replace him: something from the dark pits of a nightmare, a bestial force of hideous strength.

The two of them would run like the wind together. They would hunt and they would kill, side by side, like his dreams had been trying to tell him these last weeks. That was the way it was meant to be. . . .

*Screw that.*

Anger surging through him, jaws snapping, Tom threw himself at the slavering creature that had once been a boy like him.

## CHAPTER SEVEN

Kate crouched, petrified, at the top of the stairs. She'd waited in her room after taking her fake shower, waiting for Tom to come looking for answers. She hadn't banked on Wesley confronting him first.

So she'd stayed out of sight, eavesdropping on the pair of them, willing Wesley away so she could get to Tom, try to help him out of here.

These last weeks she'd hoped against hope that her father would make her mother see sense. After all, Tom was a silverblood—hard to turn. A natural resister. Anyone sane would've just given up on him and set him free.

But her mom wasn't sane, not any longer. What she'd done to Mark and what she'd been doing to Tom this last month had made Kate certain of that—just as she was certain now, looking at the nightmare creatures biting and snapping at each other in the room below, that she would rather die than go along with her mother's wishes.

The wolf that slept deep inside her must stay sleeping forever. She would never submit to its rule.

Tom's wolf had now fully taken him over. Kate had wanted to save his life, convinced herself she could play along. And so she'd done nothing to save him from becoming a monster.

She watched him wriggle free of the last of his clothes. His loose-limbed, rangy frame had become that of a sleek, deep-chested wolf creature covered in dark lustrous fur. He was awesome. Terrifying. In his now-lupine face, brutish jaws opened wide as a mantrap. Kate shuddered as Tom roared, his dark lips shrinking back to show off rows of dagger-sharp ivory teeth.

As she inched unnoticed down the stairs, Kate caught a glimpse of Tom's eyes. She gasped. They hadn't turned a sickly luminous yellow like Wesley's always did. Or a greenish gold like Marcie's. They had retained their deep brown, almost black color.

Still Tom's. Still human. Kate had never seen a lupine with human eyes before. What did it mean?

The two creatures circled each other slowly. Wesley, more used to his wolf form, kept rearing up on his hind legs, trying to intimidate Tom. Kate watched the muscles ripple across Tom's flank as he leapt at Wesley, snarling with rage. But her brother was too quick; he darted aside. Tom crashed down into a table, splintering it like matchwood. While he was recovering, Wesley came up behind him and sank his jaws into Tom's back. Tom's howl of agony as he tore himself free went right through Kate.

She'd assumed they were only play fighting, fooling around, that Tom was enjoying his new-found power just as Wesley had prophesied. That any moment they'd break it up, piss on the wall to mark their territory, and then chase down some mule deer in the forests outside.

But there was the familiar bloodlust in Wesley's eyes.

Tom's wolf form looked more powerful, but he was hesitant, unsure of what his new body could do. And, Kate could tell, he lacked the resolve to kill an opponent.

If Wesley didn't back down, the fight wouldn't go on much longer.

Wasn't that what she wanted? If Tom were to die, Kate's problems would be over for now. It would be Wesley's fault, not hers. And with campers in the area more vigilant since Tom's disappearance, suitable candidates would be harder for Marcie to find. Maybe Dad would even convince her to give up, to let Kate move away and have a normal life. . . .

Kate sighed, closing her eyes. She believed in werewolves because she had to. She didn't believe in any other fairy stories.

As the sounds of carnage raged on, Kate knew she had to do something.

Maybe it was time to believe in herself.


Tom's senses raced at dizzying speed. He felt immensely strong, yet weak as a kitten. It was like going from a bicycle to driving a race car—he had all this speed and power, but he lacked the experience to handle it. Just finding himself behind the wheel was awesome. The trouble was, while Tom's mind kept taking time out to marvel at the thrill and the fear of having so much bestial muscle at his command, Wesley had no such distractions. He was well used to his wolf form. And in the heat of their fighting, all that crap about the two of them being brothers seemed shot to hell.

Wesley was out for the kill.

He closed in on Tom once again, claws swiping at Tom's throat. Tom retreated, backed up against the granite fireplace, feeling the heat of the dying fire on his hind legs. As Wesley lunged for him again, Tom dodged aside. Wesley's paws sizzled as they struck the red-hot coals, and he howled with rage. The stink of burned hair and flesh caught in Tom's nostrils. He bared his teeth. He should attack now, tear flesh and snap bone, before Wesley could hurt him again.

No. No, that savagery would hurt him worse than anything Wesley could do. Tom turned away, confused and frightened. He glanced at the pile of clothes he'd been wearing, now lying ripped and empty, as if the boy inside had melted away.

Wesley reared up and smashed into his flank, pressing him down, teeth tearing at his face. Tom tried to roll free, but he was trapped, pressed down hard against the floor. He closed his eyes, hoped that when death came for him, it would be quick.

He heard something heavy scythe the air, heard the sickening impact of metal on bone.

Tom opened his eyes to find Kate backing away, brandishing a metal poker grabbed from the fireplace. Wesley was still holding him down, but his jaws had sagged dumbly open. Blood was pouring from an ugly gash in his skull.

With a low menacing growl Wesley turned from Tom to face his sister. She brandished the poker again warningly, but Tom could see the fear on her face. Kate knew as well as he did that Wesley would never give her a chance to use it again.

Wesley pounced at her. Kate shrieked. She went down under his weight, all but vanishing beneath him.

Without thinking, Tom reared forward and seized Wesley by the neck, trying to drag him away to give Kate a chance to run. Wesley twisted furiously in his grip, and Tom felt the hot tang of blood in his jaws as they broke skin. Rolling over, Wesley tried to break free. He took Tom with him, throwing him bodily into the air.

As Tom hit the ground, the impact jarred through his body. His grip on Wesley's throat tightened involuntarily. With a wet crunching sound, Wesley's windpipe was crushed between Tom's teeth like a drinking straw.

Tom pushed himself free and backed away.

Blood frothed from Wesley's sagging jaws as he clawed at his spurting throat. Kate was staring at him. She looked frightened, bewildered. Horrified.

Unable to watch any longer, Tom slunk off to a corner of the living room. He lay down, curled his body into himself for comfort. Across the room, it sounded like Wes was snoring, just asleep. Gradually the noise died away to a gentle rattle of breath. Then all Tom could hear was Kate's quiet sobs.

He couldn't tell how long the calm lasted. Spots of color started to speckle his vision. His limbs cramped up and his body shook. It felt like he was being suffocated, smothered, like the power was draining away, leaving him weak and defenseless.

Human again. Naked and bloody on a cold wooden floor.

Tom blinked, trying to clear his vision. He held up his hands, staring at the pink, hairless skin, flexing his wrists. Focusing past them, he saw Kate standing over him with a bundle of clothes and towels in her arms. Her face was unreadable as she dumped them on his chest.

"Clean yourself up and get dressed," she said quietly.

"I changed back," Tom breathed. A tear escaped the corner of his eye. "Jesus, thank God, I changed back."

Kate began to fill an empty backpack with clothing.

"You're leaving," Tom said dully. "Running away."

"We both are. Together. Tonight." Kate gestured at Wesley's body, twisted and prone beside the fireplace. "Or would you rather wait for my parents to get back so you can explain that to them?"

Tom stared at Wesley. "Is he . . . ?"

"Dead?" Kate nodded. "Yes."

"I killed him," Tom whispered. "I'm a murderer."

"You didn't mean to kill him," Kate muttered, not looking up from her backpack. "Anyway, it was self-defense."

"He's dead because of me," Tom said quietly.

"And I'm alive because of you," Kate snapped back.

Tom buried his face in his hands. "You should have let him kill me."

Kate glared at him, green eyes flashing with anger. "I'm sorry, but we don't have time for you to wallow in despair right now, okay?" She pulled out a handful of wallets stuffed with cash from the zip flap of her backpack. "Look—look at these! Wes took these from his victims. He was like my mother, out of control. He killed whenever he got the chance. These were his trophies." She zipped the wallets back inside the backpack. "The world's well rid of him."

Tom just stared at her dumbly.

"I said, clean yourself up and get dressed," Kate repeated. "Quickly. There's hot water in the kitchen."

This time Tom did as he was told. He felt as cold and mauled as the hunk of raw meat sitting in its own congealed blood on the countertop.

When he came back, Kate was shoving another bundle of jeans and T-shirts inside another back-pack. He guessed the things were Wesley's. She was dressed in a bottle green sweater and blue jeans, with well-worn Timberlands on her feet. Her black hair was tied back in a hasty ponytail that swished around her smooth, pale neck as she worked.

Tom felt for cuts on his face. "I thought I'd be more injured than I am."

"The lupine metabolism is faster," came the clipped response. "When you're 'wolf, you'll heal faster."

"When . . ." Tom shuddered. "So I'll change again?"

"Yes. But don't ask me when, because I don't know."

"I want to go home," whispered Tom.

"And lead Marcie straight to your family? So she can kill them too in revenge?" Kate shook her head, grabbed a thick winter coat, and struggled into it. "I don't think so, do you?"

"Well, where the hell *do* we go?" Tom challenged.

Kate threw a bomber jacket at his feet, hitched her backpack onto her shoulders, and walked to the front door. "Right now, anywhere but here. We hit the highway, then think about it. Are you coming?"

Dazed, Tom grabbed the other backpack and followed her outside into the cool, sweet-smelling night.

Dark clouds had diminished the moon to a glimmer, but Kate had brought a flashlight. They picked a careful path across the waterlogged causeway and soon found themselves splashing toward the edge of the forest.

Tom paused for breath. He couldn't clear his mind of the fight with Wesley, reliving every moment like a horrifically vivid dream.

"You must hate my family," Kate said quietly.

Tom saw that she was studying him. "Yes," he said simply.

Kate turned off the flashlight, to save the batteries, Tom supposed.

"I hate them too," she said. "I hate what they are and what they do." She sighed, her warm breath misting out into the night.

"When I was sick, Wesley made out like *you* were the maniac," Tom said softly. But he was determined not to feel sorry for Kate. He was the one in real trouble here. He clenched his fists, closed his eyes. "They did this to me because of you."

"I know."

"So it's your fault."

Kate's voice hardened. "You think I *want* to be married off to someone I don't even know?"

"So why didn't you help me before?"

"I tried to warn you away," Kate protested.

There was a pause. The night seemed to gather in more blackly about them.

"Don't hate me for letting it happen," Kate said.

For the first time, Tom could detect something vulnerable in her.

"I couldn't just drag you out of there; they were watching me like hawks. And you weren't in any state to jump out through the bathroom window and start running for your life." She flicked on the flashlight. It lit her angular face eerily from below. "Come on. We should get going now."

"No, wait," Tom said. "Why me? If there are thousands of werewolves, like Wesley said, and if you won't turn 'wolf till you . . ." He faltered. "Till you *do it* with one, why not pair you off with—?"

"I'll explain while we walk," Kate said resignedly.

They set off again, the conifers scratching at them like needle fingers. Each crack of a twig sounded like a car door slamming, every rustle of the undergrowth seemed to carry for miles around. Tom prayed Kate's parents weren't close by.

"Both Mom and Dad are descended from long lines of purebloodlupines—werewolves," Kate began. "Mom is a Hargrave—one of the oldest lupine families. Normally they'd do just what you said. Find a suitable boy from one of the Old Name families they wanted to strengthen ties with and lock me in a room with him. Leave a bed in there if they were feeling romantic."

Tom grimaced. "New spin on arranged marriages, huh?"

"Pureblood girls have that hanging over them from birth. As soon as they hit bloodflow, they're at risk."

"Bloodflow?" Tom frowned. "Oh, you mean when they start their—" He broke off, embarrassed. "Uh, how does it work?"

If Kate noticed his embarrassment, she didn't seem to care. "It's in the sex itself. The sweat, the proximity . . . the violation of her body and the seed placed inside it." Her voice was growing edgier. "They're taught it's the law, that it's a good thing. Maybe some of them even want to be 'wolves, I don't know. Whatever, they have no say in it. If they won't consent, they get raped."

Tom couldn't help it; he placed a hand on her shoulder. Even as she irritably shrugged him off, he could tell she was shaking.

"It's been going on for centuries," Kate said flatly, back in control. "But, as in any closed community, inbreeding causes problems. Physical deformity, proneness to disease."

Tom frowned. "Your family looked all right to me."

"Outside, maybe. But my mom is showing one of the most common symptoms: her appetite for flesh is near insatiable. She can barely control it and it's getting worse. Around the time we left Twin Falls, she was like a junkie needing her fix, pouncing on pretty much anything with a pulse and tearing it to shreds." Kate's voice sounded drained of emotion, like she'd carefully distanced herself from the meaning of her words. "It's why we had to move all the way out here, far from anywhere."

"I've sure got a lot to look forward to."

Kate sighed impatiently. "No, Tom, that's the whole point. Most werewolves keep their appetites under strict control. It's common sense. They can't just go hunting and killing all the time without attracting attention and risking the exposure of the wider werewolf community."

"So what, an injection of new blood stabilizes the gene pool or something?"

"Exactly. The purebloods take in a newblood. You have the honor of joining the noble Folan family and together we have well-behaved little 'wolves to get the clan back on track." She snorted. "Nice, huh?"

"Hey, it's cool," Tom said bitterly. "I've always

wanted someone to choose my mate and turn me into a cold-blooded killer."

"Uh-uh. I saw you fighting Wesley," Kate said firmly. "Your 'wolf is not a cold-blooded killer because Tom Anderson is not a cold-blooded killer. You're a silverblood, remember?"

"Why 'silverblood'?" he asked. Then it clicked. "Oh, right—werewolves don't like silver, isn't that it?"

Kate smiled wanly. "In the stories a silver bullet through the heart is meant to be the only way to kill a werewolf. A total myth. They can be shot dead like anyone else. The 'wolves spread that legend themselves to make humans think reaching for the shotgun was a waste of time." She snorted. "Anyway, the point is that you're a natural resister."

"So I've got to keep resisting," Tom concluded.

"Amen to that," said Kate wryly. "And I might just be able to help you in that."

He looked at her sharply. "Yeah?"

"Maybe."

They came to an unruly row of bushes blocking their way.

"You know, Kate, I . . . I'm sorry." Tom took a deep breath. "None of this is your fault. Not me . . . not Mark."

Kate said nothing for a whole minute.

"How'd it happen with him?" he prompted gently.

"Last year my tutors made me go to summer school," she said. "Help me get extra credits in

English and a shot at a college scholarship. Mother wasn't happy, but Dad overruled her. For once. Anyway, kids were there from all over the country."

"And Mark was one of them?"

"Yeah." She was quiet for a while. "I make it a rule not to get close. Never to get close, not to anyone. But stuff just . . . kind of . . . happened."

Tom nodded. "Summer romance, huh?"

"Hopeless, doomed romance, more like." She snorted softly. "Afterward, when we'd both returned home, we'd talk for hours in chat rooms online. We had so many crazy plans. . . . We figured, maybe someday when I was out of here . . ."

"Did you tell him about the wolf stuff?"

"Get real! I just said my mom and dad were total psychos about their precious darling daughter and that they'd kill him if he even came near me." Kate looked down at her boots. "Guess he didn't believe me. He tracked me down. Came all the way out here from Michigan. And since no police ever came looking, I guess he didn't tell anyone where he'd gone."

"Jeez, big mistake," muttered Tom.

"When he turned up, Mom thought the perfect opportunity had fallen into her lap, figuring I'd let him. . . ." Kate pushed out a deep breath. "So she bit him. Unlike you, he had no resistance. . . . But when I said there was no way I was going to mate with a lupine—not even him—Marcie killed him. Just like that. I couldn't believe she would just . . ."

Kate shuddered. "I wish to God I'd never even spoken to him. If I'd left him alone, it would never have happened."

"You warned him to stay away," said Tom awkwardly. "What else could you have done?"

Kate seemed not to hear him. "Marcie figured she was teaching me a lesson. Showing me she was serious. That there was no way out for me."

They stood side by side, staring at the thick, thorny tangles barring their way.

"Mark's dead. But *we're* alive, Tom." He could barely catch Kate's whisper. "We have to make that count."

Gently Tom took the flashlight from her and began skirting the thick bushes until he picked out a clearer path. Kate followed him in silence.

"You said you could help me," Tom said after a while.

"I said maybe. It means finding someone."

"Who?"

"He's not local. I'll explain once we're on the road. And try not to change again till we're well under way, all right?" Kate's voice grew still more deadpan. "You might cramp our chances. Wolf hair is a bitch to clean off car seats."

Tom guessed the joke was well meant, but right now he didn't much feel like laughing. "How come you're only running away now, anyway?" he blurted. "If *my* family were werewolves—"

"I was thirteen before I found out where Mom and Dad really went on their nights out," Kate cut in. "Once I knew, I ran away almost every month. I only stopped when Mom threatened to bring one of my friends home for dinner." She paused and Tom could see her fighting to retain her calm. "If you know what I mean."

"And the situation's different now?" Tom asked.

"Well, I don't make friends anymore. At least, not the kind of friends Mom can find. The kids at school think I'm a freak or super-shy or something. I spend a lot of time online at the school computer center. Chat rooms, Web rings . . . you know."

"Pretty lonely, huh."

"Sometimes. But when I met Mark, I just couldn't resist the opportunity to get close to someone. Just for a while." She gave a short, bitter laugh. "Who was I kidding?"

Tom hesitated before speaking again. "Your mom . . . she's not going to stop looking for us, is she?"

"No," said Kate simply. "She and Dad will put out the word. There are werewolf packs all over the country. They look after their own."

"But if your mom was some kind of high-risk werewolf pain in the ass who had to go into hiding, why would they help her?"

"'Wolf is 'wolf." Kate sighed. "The bonds go deep. And she's one of the Old Names. That counts for a lot. Besides, a lot of 'wolves feel the same way she does: why *should* they curb their behavior?" She paused. "Anyway. With or without help, after all the effort she put into turning you, she's not about to let you slip away."

"But if I could find a cure . . ." Tom knew he was like a dog with a bone, but he couldn't stop himself. "Kate, please, tell me more about this help."

"First things first," Kate said briskly. "We should come to the highway soon."

They trudged on, a little faster now that the trees were starting to thin out. Tom made a couple of stumbling attempts at conversation, but Kate seemed to prefer silence. Well, that was okay for her, Tom thought. She'd had years to live with this crap. So much had happened tonight, he didn't know what to worry about first.

Finally they reached the highway, a gloomy stretch of asphalt snaking up into the hills. Tom checked his watch. Wesley had said his parents would be back around dawn. Now it was 3:20 a.m. The sane world was asleep, but Tom was too scared to be tired.

He wondered if he would ever sleep again.

"Stay at the side of the road," Kate ordered, and quickly shucked off her backpack and coat. Soon she was tugging at her sweater, too.

"Are—are you crazy?" Tom stammered, bewildered. "It's freezing; you'll catch your—"

"Death?" He heard rather than saw her wry smile. "I'm hoping to get us a ride." She pulled off her sweater. Beneath it was a flimsy vest top. "*You* don't have to stare," she told him firmly. "Get out of sight."

Tom turned back to the bushes, baffled and embarrassed.

"It's not a very sociable time for traveling," she reminded him, pulling her coat back on. "If a man sees a girl dressed like this at the side of the road, he'll be quicker to stop if you're *not* standing next to me, don't you think?"

He made a big show of considering this. "Maybe you should lose the jeans as well."

"Watch it," Kate told him. "Or I might just hitch that ride and take off *without* my bodyguard."

Tom grinned. Then he realized just what she'd said.

"Bodyguard?" he echoed darkly. "Oh, I get it."

Kate looked down at the ground awkwardly. "Get what?"

"That's why you brought me along, isn't it?" Tom snarled. "You stand a better chance of getting away with a tame 'wolf on your side."

"It's not that, you idiot!" she hissed. "Not *just* that. We can look out for each other! Right now I'm all you've got."

Tom sneered. "That crap you spouted about being able to help. It comes down to this? Feeding me some bull about a cure to stop me from running off too soon?"

"Keep your voice down!" Kate urged him. "Tom, I really do think there's someone who might be able to help you, okay?"

He wanted to believe her.

But then, he'd believed Marcie Folan when she'd said he was getting better.

"Good luck, Kate. See you around."

Leaving Kate alone at the edge of the forest, Tom turned and walked off down the highway. Somewhere, miles up ahead, was the winding path that led down to that little group of log cabins for hire. Bitter tears welled up. If he could only go back to that morning when he'd walked away from his family and this time live it differently. Keep his mouth shut instead of arguing. Would it have killed him to be the dutiful son for a week? Just to hug his mom again, see his dad's smile, or swing Joe through the air by his ankles. Joe used to love that. . . .

He stopped. He couldn't see his hand in front of his face. The path ahead was pitch black. The kind of path monsters would take.

And there was nothing for him down that road now, anyway.

Somewhere distant he heard the whine of an approaching car. He glanced back at Kate. She was standing right where he left her, watching him. Her flashlight made a pool of weak light around her feet. It wasn't much, but it was something.

Tom turned and walked back to her as the noise of the car grew louder. "Guess it's time to try out your hitching theory."

Kate stepped out into the road, let her coat fall open. "Guess it is," she said, glancing back at him. She held out her thumb.

The car rolled by, ignoring her. They waited quietly for the next car to come, together.

## CHAPTER EIGHT

It took over an hour, but at last a dented Ford Taurus stopped for them. A woman in her forties with big messy hair waved them over with a silly grin. She smelled of booze and cigarettes. "I'm going as far as Goldendale," she announced. "That suit you?"

Kate looked at Tom and he saw a flicker of hope in her face. "That's clear across Washington State! From there we can take the Greyhound."

"Take it where?" Tom asked as he slid into the backseat after her.

"I'll tell you later," Kate replied. Then she whispered, looking at the woman, "Trust me. No one else."

"I was supposed to drive on down to meet up with my husband this afternoon," said the woman in a three-packs-a-day voice, "only a little party I threw got out of hand." She cackled. "You kids been partying too?"

"You could say that," Kate said wryly.

"Well, I'm gunning this engine all the way to

make up lost time," she said. To prove her point, she floored the gas, and the tires screeched horribly as the car shot away.

Tom wondered what kind of sound Marcie would make when she found her son dead and himself and Kate gone.

The car rolled on. The vents whooshed out hot air. Soon Tom fell into a deep and dreamless sleep.

The day came and went in drowsy snatches. Tom's eyes opened on beige vinyl upholstery . . . a clear blue sky out of the fogged-up window . . . a Taco Bell drive-through, the waitress's voice squawking out of the loudspeaker . . . Kate's hair spilling down over her shoulders. Her face turned away from him, staring out of the window.

Then it was dark.

Tom woke up in a strange room. Grimy net curtains swelled into the room as the breeze caught them. The wallpaper was busy with faded flowers.

He was stripped to his boxers, sweating and shivering under a flimsy quilt in a narrow bed.

With a low moan he rolled out of bed, scrabbled at the sheet, certain of what he would see. But the wolf pelt wasn't back beneath him. The lumpy mattress was stained but bare.

He jumped as a door to his right opened.

It was Kate, her hair bundled up into a baseball

cap, wearing a baggy shirt and pants. She held a brown bag of groceries in the crook of her arm and was looking at him oddly. "You okay?"

Tom nodded. "I guess."

"You had a fever." She set down the groceries and started to tuck the corner of his sheet back under the mattress. "Could be your body fighting against whatever my mother's been spooning down your throat for the last month. Or it could be withdrawal symptoms."

"Thanks, Nurse." Tom stumbled over to the window, hoping for some fresh air, but caught instead a lungful of car exhaust from the busy street outside. "Where are we?"

"Goldendale. Delivered as the lady promised."

He stared at her. "Already?"

Kate snorted. "It took forever! You may have been sick, but at least you slept through all her gross stories about swinging parties and stuff."

Tom grimaced. "How long was I out for?"

"All day. I've checked us into a motel for tonight." She pulled out two Cup Noodles and flicked the switch on a battered kettle. "Hungry?"

He gave her a tight smile. "If it's vegetarian."

She read the label. "Sweet and sour."

"Sounds like the two of us." He smiled properly this time. "Though I guess you do have your sweet moments, too."

Kate mimed sticking her fingers down her throat.

Tom blushed. "Seriously. Thanks for taking care of me."

"Runs in the family, I guess. Just don't count on *me* doing it for a month."

Tom turned away angrily. "You know what? Screw you."

"Hey." Kate sat beside him softly. "Sorry. I've spent the last three years living in chat rooms. I keep thinking you can see the emotions when I speak."

Tom turned to her. "Huh?"

"You know. 'Colon-dash–right parenthesis' equals smiley face. 'Semicolon-dash–right parenthesis' equals winking smiley face. 'This is me joking, so don't take offense.'" She pulled the relevant faces for him. "All that stuff."

Tom nodded and managed a halfhearted smiley face of his own. But his attention was taken more by the way Kate's pale green eyes seemed to glitter even in a dingy motel room.

The kettle clicked off and she turned away. She poured boiling water into the Cup Noodles, stirred them with a teaspoon, and passed one to him. "Peace offering."

They shoveled down the noodles in hungry silence.

When she'd finished, Kate passed him a ticket from her purse. "Better rest up, sick boy. The bus leaves at five o'clock tomorrow and it's a long trip."

Tom drained the last of his noodles. "Where to?"

"New Orleans."

"But that's, like, twenty-five hundred miles away!" He frowned. "Why New Orleans?"

"Because . . ." She leaned forward, an amused smile on her lips. "Jicaque."

*Zhi-cah-key?* "Bless you." Tom raised an eyebrow. "You know, it's hard to look mysterious when you have a noodle sauce mustache."

She pulled away and made a funny noise. He realized it was the first real laugh he'd heard from her.

"So what's Jicaque?" he asked as Kate wiped her mouth and checked her reflection. "Sounds like it should be a chili dip or something."

"*It* is a *he*. Supposed to be some kind of medicine man or witch doctor," Kate said. "I heard he lives in New Orleans somewhere. And that he can cure newbloods, if they've been turned recently enough."

"Cure?" Tom's heart leapt. "So you weren't kidding me about being able to help? This guy is real? Really real?"

"Whoa. This won't be easy, Tom," Kate cautioned. "I have no idea where in New Orleans he's supposed to live—or what he looks like. And we can't exactly go around asking for directions to the local witch doctor. . . ."

Tom slumped back down on the bed. "How did you hear about him, anyway?"

She shrugged. "Conversations online. Years

spent posting to paranormal newsgroups or speaking in chat rooms with people who've lived through all kinds of weird stuff."

"Sounds like fun," Tom remarked lightly.

"Hey." Kate's lip had curled down in disapproval. "I'm sure you're Mr. Totally Straight, but my whole life's been an X-file, okay? Only there's no cute FBI agent coming to save *my* day. Pardon me if I need to talk to people who *don't* think I'm totally nuts or delusional."

"Okay, okay!" Tom said quickly. "Jicaque. New Orleans. Thanks. It's a start."

Kate nodded. "We can find an Internet café on the way. I can look up some of my old e-friends and try to get the latest on him."

Tom sighed. "It's going to take us days to get there by bus."

"Uh-huh. But it's safer than hitching." She yawned noisily. "We don't know who's waiting and watching out there."

"You want the bed?" asked Tom.

"Yeah." Her willowy body arched gracefully as she stretched. "You thought I made it for *you?* Get real, sick boy. You get the couch."

She kicked off her boots and pulled herself beneath the covers fully clothed without another word.

Tom took a spare blanket and sprawled on the couch. He watched TV with the sound turned down, listening to her breathing grow deeper, more rhythmic. But he couldn't relax. He flicked endlessly from Cartoon Network to CNN, each time convinced he'd see some headline screaming NEW SEATTLE BOY MURDER: COPS HUNT KILLERS or Marcie Folan's face filling the screen, weeping at a press conference with a big picture of Wesley smiling cutely out from behind her.

The moon was up high in the sky, and he could feel himself sweating. He told himself to stay calm. Every minute, every hour, right through the sleepless night.


The next day passed just as slowly as they waited for five o'clock to roll around. They couldn't go out and risk being seen, and besides, the bus tickets had been pricey. They needed a cheap day.

For *cheap*, read *dull*. Tom had won and lost the jackpot on every slot machine in the lobby three times over. Now he had to keep trooping back over to Kate, the money holder, to cadge quarters. It was a ritual that annoyed them both.

"Why can't you just give me one of the wallets?" Tom asked irritably.

Kate shook her head. "If you go 'wolf on me and lose your clothes, we lose the money."

"Thanks for your faith in me," Tom said sourly. "Maybe pissing me off like this is more likely to *make* me go 'wolf."

Kate ignored him, burying her nose back in some old book she was pretending to read.

The quarters ran out in the end. To make up the deficit, they sneaked out of a diner without paying for their coffee.

"Can you believe we did that?" Tom gasped once they'd reached the next block and declared themselves in the clear.

"First we kill a creature from ancient mythology, then we steal coffee," said Kate dryly. "America's most wanted."

Now they were hanging out at the bus station, butts numb from the metal bench. The Greyhound dog stared out at them from posters and rumbling bus sides. Vagrants rummaged through trash cans; people hugged and kissed hello and goodbye.

Tom imagined his own family alighting from one of the buses, finding him waiting here. Grabbing him in for a hug and not letting go. He glanced over at a pay phone for the tenth time.

"Don't even think about it," Kate warned him, looking up from her book. "The first thing Mom will do is track down your folks and have them watched. If you get in touch, establish any kind of contact . . . she'll use them to get to you."

A terrible thought occurred to Tom. "What's to stop her from getting them anyway?"

"I don't think she'd risk the manhunt that would cause," reasoned Kate. "I mean, first you missing in strange circumstances, then your whole family? Uh-uh. Easier to chase the guy who's already dead."

Tom found he was grinding his teeth. "Well, can't we go to the cops anonymously, just in case? Warn them my family could be in danger?"

Kate looked at him like he was a moron or something. "You think there aren't 'wolves in the police? In the mayor's office? In the courts? Anywhere a useful blind eye might be turned?"

"You're kidding me," Tom said uneasily.

"Over eight hundred thousand people were reported missing to the FBI last year," Kate said. "They're still missing. Mysterious, huh?"

"Okay," Tom snarled. "Enough said." He looked across at her. "What are you reading, anyway? That book looks like it came out of the Ark."

"It's a volume of ancient werewolf lore and rituals," Kate said quietly. "I'm trying to find out all I can about silverbloods."

"Guess that's the kind of homework I should be doing, huh?"

"Some of us read. Some of us whine." Kate added a quick smile and stuck out her tongue.

Tom sighed. "So what does it say?" he asked.

"That fever is quite common in the newly turned. Plus there's interesting stuff about something called a *wereling*."

"Which is?"

"A particular type of silverblood. Very rare."

"So?"

"Okay. Skipping the 'thee's and 'thou's, a wereling is a resister whose humanity and compassion prevail in the 'wolf. Pureblood hard-liners despise werelings as useless to the pack; liberals appreciate their rarity, see in them the perfect synthesis of man and wolf." She paused, looking at Tom questioningly, then continued. "In one of the old myths there's mention of a wereling arriving in the world around the dawn of Wolf Time. Depending on who you believe, he can be the savior of the 'wolf race—or its destroyer."

Tom felt cold alarm creeping over him. "And you think that I could be . . ."

Kate couldn't keep her face straight any longer and dissolved in low giggles.

Tom relaxed. "Bitch!" he said incredulously, but he was grinning too.

"They're just old stories," Kate said. "No one really believes them."

Suddenly there was a loud cry to their left. Tom jumped up, grabbing hold of Kate's hand, ready to run. But all they saw was a young woman in a head scarf, staring around frantically, her hand to her mouth.

"My baby," she gasped. "I went to get some change, and now . . ." She started shouting: "Bobby! Bobby, honey, where are you?"

"What did he look like?" Tom asked.

Kate pulled her hand away and jabbed him in

the ribs. "We're not drawing attention to ourselves," she hissed, nodding at the crowd gathering around the woman. "Remember?"

"He's three years old, big for his age, with sandy hair . . ." the woman began.

As she went on with her description, Tom saw a half-eaten crustless sandwich in the child's stroller. Concentrating, he could smell the peanut-butter-and-grape-jelly filling. He turned in a slow circle, trying to see if he could scent it anywhere else.

Kate tried to pull him away. "Stay out of this, Tom," she warned him. "You don't know if she's for real."

"I can smell him," Tom breathed. "Wait here."

"Don't leave me!" Kate panicked.

"Just a few seconds," Tom promised her. Then he jogged across the concourse, sniffing the air. It was like he could home in on the scent of the little boy, and it was mingling now with the overwhelming stench of . . .

Tom hurried to the men's room, and there was Bobby, grinning as his sandy brown hair was buffeted in the blast from a hot-air dryer.

"I needed to go pee," the pudgy little boy announced.

"When you gotta go, you gotta go," Tom agreed. He picked him up and carried him back across the concourse. He smelled like soap and candy, safe and clean. The way Joe used to smell. Tom had resented having a baby brother so much at the start, but . . .

He froze.

The smell of the plump little boy in his arms was making him salivate.

"Here," Tom muttered, dumping Bobby in his mother's arms without another word.

"Thanks," the woman called gratefully, but Tom was already walking away. The crowd began to disperse.

Kate appeared, carrying his backpack as well as her own. "What am I, the bellhop now?"

Tom slumped down on another bench, sank his face into his hands. "I . . . I thought maybe I could find something good in all this mess," he whispered. "That I could help."

"You did help," Kate said softly, joining him. "You were right about the boy and you sniffed him out."

Tom snorted. "I wanted to *eat* him."

"But you *didn't*," Kate said quietly. "You drew on the wolf in you without letting it out. I've never seen that before." She smiled at him. "Hey, wereling. Perfect synthesis of man and wolf . . ."

"There's nothing perfect about me," Tom snapped. "What if next time that hunger hits me, I *can't* control it? Can't stop myself?"

Kate was silent for a long moment. "Come on," she said at last. "It's almost five. We should get ready to board."

Tom closed his eyes. You didn't need to be Einstein to know why Kate hadn't answered his question. She didn't *have* an answer.

# CHAPTER NINE

The journey through Oregon passed slowly. By midnight they were nearing the town of Ontario. The bus was comfortable enough, but Tom was miserable and preoccupied, too restless to settle.

The moon glowed slyly in through the thin curtain Kate had dragged across the window. Tom's face itched and tickled in its faint light. "You don't think I'll change, do you?" he whispered to Kate for the twelfth time.

She didn't look up from her book. "Tom, if I knew, I promise I would tell you."

He sank farther down in his seat. "The moon's not even full anymore."

Kate sighed. "The moon is a big influence on werewolves *all* the time. The reason the full moon is associated with them most is because it's the 'wolf Sabbath. A day of ancient rituals. Now come on, Tom, try to relax."

"I can't." He shook his head, pushed back his dark hair with sweaty fingers. "I feel like if I just let myself go I could slip over the edge. Can you imagine what I might do to these people?"

"Yes," said Kate simply. "Listen, we hit Twin Falls in a little while. Happy homecoming to me."

"Great." He snorted. "I can take on anyone your mom missed."

"No, you won't," she told him flatly. "And since my mom ran amok there, kicking up all that fuss, I don't think any other self-respecting 'wolf would go there either."

"Not till Wolf Time, right?" Tom sighed. "What *is* that, anyway?"

Giving up on her book, Kate slapped its yellowed pages shut. "Okay. Wolf Time. It's a time described in an epic poem called *Das Zeitalter des Werwolfs*—in which werewolves gain dominion over the world. Full of werewolf warriors, strange portents and signs in the sky, destiny, the overthrowing of humanity, coming out of the shadows and bathing in the blood of man, yada yada yada . . . It's a big thing in werewolf literature—some see it as prophetic of a real time to come."

"Werewolf literature?" Tom looked at her skeptically. "Maybe I could major in that when I get into Princeton."

"A lot of it's actually beautifully written, in a sick kind of way," Kate said.

Tom rolled his eyes. Like he'd been serious. Kate was happy to dish out the sarcasm but never seemed to see it herself.

"*Das Zeitalter des Werwolfs* is a good example," she continued. "It's German, seventeenth century. The author's unknown."

"I guess it's sort of the werewolf version of *Planet of the Apes*," said Tom, earning himself an I-give-up look from Kate.

"It's all a bunch of crap, anyway," she said dismissively. "No one really believes it. I mean, they'd *like* to . . . but then, I'd like to believe in the tooth fairy. What can you do?" Kate turned back to her book.

Tom saw that the subject of Wolf Time was officially closed.

Soon bored and edgy again, he turned his attention to their fellow passengers. Trying to distract himself, he focused on the sounds around him, zeroing in on different voices. He smiled wickedly. He could do it, too—tune in to intimate conversations like they were secret live broadcasts going on all around him. If anyone *was* tailing him and Kate, maybe he'd hear something that would give them away.

After "station hopping" from a woman going on about her vacation photos to a man talking about the problems he was having with his boss, Tom listened in on two guys a few seats behind him.

*"Take it now."*

*"Not yet."*

*"Now, while the dumb bitch is sleeping, go on."*

Tom grew instantly alert. The guys had boarded

at the last stop and had looked innocuous enough. But clearly they weren't. . . .

Casually he turned around, like he'd dropped something. He saw that the elderly black woman seated behind him had fallen asleep. The over-stuffed bag lying on the empty seat next to her had fallen open, revealing a thick roll of banknotes wedged in a side pocket.

Tom looked away. Maybe they wouldn't really do it. He kept on listening.

*"Do it now! She won't notice until we're gone."*

One of the guys got up from his seat. Tom's mind raced through his options. He could wake the old woman, or he could just turn around and stare at the guy, show him he'd been seen. The guy would probably back down.

But instead Tom got up, grabbed hold of the man's neck, and bared his teeth.

Passengers yelled in alarm, and the man shrank back, shocked and frightened. "Whoa, man," he gasped, trying to pry Tom's fingers from his neck. "Get the hell off me!"

Tom shook his head. He couldn't stop. And he couldn't speak. Every word he tried to form came out as a growl.

Kate grabbed hold of him, pulling on his arm. The thief's friend stood up on his seat, shouting out threats from a safe distance.

The bus driver slammed on the brakes.

The jolt seemed to bring Tom back to his senses. He slackened his grip and the thief staggered back to his friend, clutching his neck.

"Next stop's Caldwell, mister," the driver called to Tom down the aisle. "Will you return to your seat or do I dump you right here?"

"He's fine, and we're sorry," Kate called as she guided Tom back to his seat. "All a big misunderstanding; everything's cool." In his ear she hissed angrily: "You're acting like a total freak! What *is* it?"

"He was going to steal her money," Tom muttered, pointing to the old woman. "I had to stop him. . . ."

"Oh, my, I believe you're right, young man," the old woman said. The disturbance had woken her, and she was smiling gratefully at him. "I dozed off without shutting my bag. Again . . ." She sighed. "Crazy old fool, leaving my money in the open that way. If I'd lost it, I couldn't eat for a month." She placed a warm, wrinkled hand on Tom's leg. "Thank you *so* much."

"It's okay," Tom muttered.

"I reckon that's more than can be said for you." The old woman looked at him with some concern. "What's wrong?"

Tom hesitated, floundering for a plausible excuse for his feverish appearance. "Just tired, I guess," he said finally, forcing a smile.

The woman nodded sympathetically. "My name's

103

Patience Stern," she introduced herself. "I used to be a midwife. Once a nurse, always a nurse, I guess." The laughter lines scrunched up around her warm brown eyes. "You kids got far to go? Where you going?"

Tom opened his mouth to tell her, but Kate gave him a warning look.

"What it is . . ." She laughed awkwardly and took Tom's hand. "We're actually eloping. Traveling around, seeing where life takes us . . ." she added vaguely.

Tom's mouth stayed open.

"Our parents say we're too young, but what do they know about it, huh?" said Kate conspiratorially.

*What do I know about it?* thought Tom dazedly. He found he liked the feeling of Kate's slim hand in his.

Patience was lapping this up. "That is so adorable!" she squealed, beaming with delight. "So, you got a place to stay tonight?"

"Oh, we thought we'd just stay on the bus—keep going, y' know," Kate told her.

Patience clucked like a mother hen. Then she pursed her lips and nodded, like she'd come to a conclusion. "Look, you two, I get off at the next stop. And since my youngest moved out fifteen years back—I've been staying with him this week, you know—I can easily give two lovebirds a night's lodgings."

Kate shook her head. "Oh no, we couldn't really—"

"Now, I insist!" Patience folded her arms across

her ample bosom. "After all, one good turn deserves another. I'll give you a bed for the night and send you on your way with a good breakfast." She looked meaningfully at Tom. "Be a lot better for him than staying cooped up here on the bus all night."

Tom felt the itch tickling through his body again. The moon was still gloating at him through the window. "She's right," he muttered.

Kate looked at him, troubled, then back to Patience. "That's really nice of you, thanks. Would you mind if we talked about it?"

"Sure, honey," Patience agreed, settling back in her seat. "You go right ahead."

Kate immediately snatched her hand from Tom's and absently curled her long hair around her fingers. "Thanks, but no thanks," she muttered.

"Kate, I have to get out of here," Tom whispered. "What if I lose control again? Or worse this time?"

"Your body's fighting the 'wolf infection. It'll pass." She sighed. "And we don't know Patience from Eve. Why should she want to help us?"

Tom gave her a withering look. "Out in the real world it's called returning a favor. I saved her money, now she's offering us a bed for the night." He put a hand on Kate's leg as Patience had done to him and tried to smile. *"Fiancée."*

"You want to talk about favors?" Kate said, ignoring him. "If she's seen with us, we could be marking her out for death. Did you think about that?"

"All right, whatever." Tom groaned. He wriggled uncomfortably in his seat, his head starting to pound. "But I have to get off at Caldwell. Even if we just wait at the station for the next bus. I can't sit here any longer."

Kate nodded. "Okay. I'll tell Patience we'll skip the bed and breakfast." She rose up in her seat. Then she stopped, smiled, and nudged Tom.

Patience was asleep again, snoring quietly to herself, her bulging purse lying open again on her lap.

When the bus pulled into Caldwell, Tom almost fell out of the doors. The backpack seemed to weigh twice as much as it did before. And always the itch was prickling through his veins, tickling the back of his mind until he wanted to scream.

High above, the moon gleamed silver in the black sky. Tom gave it the finger and shuffled over to the sidewalk. "Wish I knew how long this was going to last," he croaked.

"Me too, believe me," said Kate. Her manner was brusque, but he could see that she was troubled. Afraid for him or afraid for herself?

Patience heaved herself off the bus and waved to them. She was the only other person alighting here. She hesitated as she turned to leave the terminal. "Sure there's nothing I can do for you two?"

Kate bit her lip, looking worriedly at Tom. "If anyone comes for us while you're like this, we'll be helpless."

Tom said nothing.

Kate made a decision. "Uh, Patience?" she called. "If the offer still stands . . ."

Kate felt horribly exposed as they shuffled slowly through the dark streets. Patience must have been in her sixties, but she was actually walking faster than Tom could manage. He had to keep asking them to stop and rest. It was driving Kate mad.

And, clichéd though she knew it was, she couldn't shake the feeling they were being watched.

One time, while Tom rested against a lamppost, still shivering and sweating, Patience sidled over to Kate. "Listen, honey," she said in a low voice. "Your boy. He . . . he isn't using, is he?"

Kate blinked in surprise and found herself smiling. "Tom? No way. He's so straight he'd get flashbacks from a strong cup of coffee."

Patience looked relieved. "Good. I don't approve of that kind of thing. Drugs and all." She looked up at Kate uncertainly. "I *can* trust the pair of you, can't I?"

"Yes, you can," Kate replied gently. "How about we pay you what we can for board? I'm sure Tom will feel better after some sleep. We'll be out of your hair first thing in the morning."

Patience beamed again. "No rush. And I'll drive you back to the terminal in my old Chevy."

"Really, there's no need—"

"It'll be a pleasure," Patience declared brightly as they all shuffled off again. "Little spin'll be good for it. Poor car's shut away out of sight most of the time. . . ."

While the old woman chattered on, Kate lost herself in her thoughts. She was acting so cool in front of Tom, playing it like she was some tough bitch who knew just what she was doing. Luckily he didn't seem to realize how terrified she really was.

How many times had she lain alone in her room, imagining this kind of freedom? But could she hack it in the real world? She'd spent most of the last three years avoiding other people's company, too scared to let anyone get close to her for fear of what her family might do to them. And Mark's fate, after he'd slipped through her radar, had proved her right. Back in her room, when she'd gotten tired of someone, she'd just said, "Bye!" and turned them off, disconnected. So clean and simple. Now, suddenly, here she was, cooped up for days with a guy she barely knew, in her face the whole time.

Not clean. Not simple.

She shot a glance at Tom, shuffling and shaking along the pavement beside her like he had Parkinson's or something. Wereling or not, this wasn't running away. It was wading through molasses. Kate felt a surge of panic, claustrophobia, and agoraphobia all mixed up together.

Tom caught her eyes on him. He straightened a little, forced a smile.

Kate looked away guiltily. Back when she'd thought he was leaving her all alone at the edge of the forest, in the aftermath of that awful, sickening violence, she'd wanted to scream for him to come back. Now she felt like screaming at him to leave her the hell alone. It wasn't fair and she knew it, just like all the horrible things he'd gone through weren't fair. But behind the tough bitch was a frightened little girl who felt like she was suffocating.

*Ditch him,* that part of her urged. *Sneak out tonight while he's sleeping and disappear. Hide away where they'll never find you.*

"I said, we're *here,* honey." Patience looked at her oddly, then smiled. "You seemed miles away."

Kate gave Patience a weak smile back. *I wish,* she thought.

They were standing outside a dilapidated clapboard bungalow. Home sweet home. Tom clung to the porch rail like he'd fall if he let go. Patience unlocked the door and gestured them inside. Tom muttered thank-yous as he went inside, but Kate paused on the threshold.

"You two had a fight?" Patience queried. "You haven't said a word to each other all the way here."

"It's nothing, really," said Kate, suddenly exhausted.

"Then I'd kiss and make up if I were you," Patience advised sympathetically. "Looks to me like that boy needs you right now, honey."

Kate sighed. "I guess maybe he does."

Patience fed them some eggs and toast, then went off to prepare her spare room.

Poor old Patience—well named, Tom observed. She'd made some game stabs at conversation while they were eating, but with him shivering on the couch and Kate quiet and withdrawn in a chair, it was pretty hopeless.

After a few minutes Patience had called them in, bid them sweet dreams, then retired to her own room.

Tom gratefully tugged the heavy drapes across the window, shutting out the moon's bald glare, and then surveyed their digs for the night. He and Kate faced each other awkwardly over the single bed.

"I know we're almost married, but . . ." Tom felt himself flushing. "How about we go head to toe?"

"You take it," Kate told him. "I'll take the floor."

"Doesn't seem very gallant of me," Tom observed.

"It isn't." She took a blanket from the bed. "But you're sick and I'm saintly."

"Too sick to argue, that's for sure." He tugged absently at his shirt. "I don't even have the strength to get changed for sleep."

He waited for a smart remark, but Kate stayed

silent. She just kicked off her boots and flopped down on the blanket fully clothed.

Tom was uneasy as he lay back on the bed. He knew Kate coped with the world by keeping it at arm's length and throwing sarcasm at it, but there was something restless in her manner now. She couldn't look him in the eye.

He was still puzzling as sleep broke over him silently, like a black wave.

Tom woke with a spasm of cramp in his legs. It was still dark. He rubbed at his calf muscles, swung them over the side of the bed. And froze.

His fever had gone. But so had Kate. If she were still lying down, his feet would be in her face right now.

He switched on the bedside light, and his uneasy feeling grew stronger. Kate's backpack had vanished with her.

Suddenly wide awake, the cramp in his legs forgotten, Tom pulled on his shoes and opened the door a crack. It gave onto the little living room. The clutter and bric-a-brac made strange shapes and shadows in the orange gloom spilled by the street-lights outside. "Kate?" he whispered.

Nothing.

*"Kate!"*

The toilet flushed. Tom relaxed a little and waited for her to return. But it was Patience who shuffled into the living room through the other door, wrapped up in a robe, her feet buried in fluffy slippers.

"What's up?" she asked, turning on a floor lamp. "Thought I heard you call for Kate. You telling me you managed to lose your bride-to-be in that itty-bitty room?"

Tom guessed he couldn't blame her for being suspicious. "Uh, no, I just—that is . . ." Tom smiled awkwardly, unsure quite what to say and not wanting to alarm her any further. "Sorry, I was just, uh . . . trying to wake her. But she's flat out." Or *out,* anyway, he thought worriedly.

"You're all dressed. Not planning on leaving without saying goodbye, I hope?"

He shook his head, smiled politely, his mind elsewhere.

"Couldn't sleep, huh?" Patience sank down in an old armchair. "Well, I know sleepless. And restless." She chuckled. "Yeah, they're both old friends of mine. I know how it feels to be cooped up with too little space and too much hunger. . . ." Then her voice hardened. "And I know who you are and what you've done. Both of you."

Tom's face froze in shock. Gooseflesh rose along his arms and neck.

"Just as I knew some punk would try to steal my money on the bus if they thought I was asleep. And that a nice boy like you would jump to my rescue without suspecting a thing."

Tom stared in horror at the dark shape in the chair as it started to shake.

"Marcie's put out the word on you two." Patience's kind features gave way to something twisted and feral. Her eyes shone yellow-white like the moon through the gloom of the room. Her back arched and snapped; she fell forward. The robe dropped away to reveal thick, silver-gray fur covering her skin like mold on a peach.

"Payback time," she snarled. Her face bent and cracked outward into a snout; her jaws sagged to reveal long, yellowing teeth. And all that had been human was consumed by 'wolf.

# CHAPTER TEN

Tom backed away. He grabbed a throw from the old armchair and tossed it at the nightmare creature creeping toward him. She leapt easily to one side to dodge it. Tom's heart sank further as he circled away from her—and away from both the front door and his stuff in the spare room. Despite her age, the werewolf that had been Patience Stern was fast. Tom debated whether or not he could reach the door that led through to the rest of the bungalow before she could stop him.

It would be close.

A desperate idea came to him. Tom looked past Patience to the doorway of the spare room. "Kate, get back, quick!" he shouted.

As the 'wolf spun around eagerly, Tom darted for the internal door.

Patience roared as she realized she had been tricked and bounded after him. Tom slammed the door shut in her face. A second later he heard claws on the wood, heavy paws swiping at the handle.

"Kate!" he called, terrified, pushing back against the door with all his weight. "Kate, are you here?" No answer save the pounding on the door, which boomed and shook as Patience hurled her lupine bulk against it.

*She's gone,* he realized with a sick feeling. *Isn't it obvious? She ditched me the first chance she got.*

Tom stared around frantically at the small passageway that led to the only other rooms in the place: Patience's bedroom, the bathroom, and the kitchen.

There was a back door in the kitchen.

Tom grabbed a wooden chair from the kitchen and wedged it under the living-room-door handle. Then he dashed to the back door.

He caught a glimpse of yellow eyes through the grimy glass of the window. Crouched shapes slunk back into the shadows.

Patience had called her friends. No escape that way, then.

Tom ran to the cluttered bathroom, yanking the frayed light cord as he entered. He stood panting under the light of the bare bulb. THUD! THUD! The wooden door frame began to splinter as Patience slammed it again.

There was a black rectangle of frosted glass above the toilet. The window looked just big enough for him to squeeze through—

He jumped back and swore as the window

cracked under the weight of something heavy from outside. Something was trying to get inside, to get him. He backed away and caught his leg against the bathtub, teetered forward, and fell inside along with bottles of bath salts. Cursing, he scrambled back out and, out of options, dived straight inside Patience's bedroom and slammed the door.

Then he heard the low growl and saw the old gray 'wolf rising from behind the bed, jaws wet and open, eyes shining in triumph. She must have gotten through the living room door while he'd been knocking stuff into the tub. Crept in here and waited for him, *playing* with him, knowing that this was the only place he could go.

But he guessed the fooling around was over.

Tom's heart beat hard enough to punch a hole in his ribs. He wondered if the wolf inside him, sensing death close at hand, would rise up and fight. He gritted his teeth, prayed it would stay hidden and die with him, alone in its own darkness.

Patience's powerful leg muscles tensed. She was about to jump, when the whole of the far wall seemed to collapse in an explosion of brick and sheetrock. Tom threw his arms over his face for protection and fell back against the door. The old 'wolf squealed as debris piled down on her.

Giant yellow eyes shone through the dust as something huge roared and screeched into the room.

It was a blue Chevy, skewed headlights glaring out from its bashed-in front. Hadn't Patience said she owned a—?

"Get in, you idiot!"

Through the cloud of thick dust Tom made out Kate's form behind the wheel. "What the—?"

"Quick!" she snapped, checking the rearview mirror. "There are 'wolves everywhere!"

Tom scrambled across the rubble to reach the passenger door. Patience, still in her wolf form, was whimpering, bloodied and half crushed beneath a pile of brick and plaster.

He jumped over her with a shudder, flung open the door, and slid into the seat beside Kate. "Nice driving."

"It wasn't," she remarked, pumping the pedals and grappling with the gearshift. "I didn't mean to crash through the wall. I got the brake and accelerator mixed up." A metallic rasp belched across the sound of the idling engine. "Jesus. Where the hell is reverse . . . ?"

"Look out!" Tom shouted. A shape had detached itself from the shadows outside the pool of the car's headlights, a monster bounding toward them so fast he could barely track it.

"Finally!" Kate cried as the car lurched backward.

The werewolf threw itself onto the car, landing with an impact that might have shattered the suspension. It scrabbled for a hold as Kate reversed the

Chevy at sickening speed. As she went careering out onto the quiet suburban road, the beast's front claws actually punctured the metal of the hood, securing it while its back paws scrabbled to find a hold.

Kate stomped on the brake. The car bucked to a halt. Tom's hand met hers trembling on the gearshift.

The 'wolf craned its neck, its jaws snapping at them through the windshield, its breath clouding up the glass.

"Hit the gas!" Tom yelled, and rammed the shift into drive. Wheels spinning, the Chevy screeched forward. But the 'wolf clung on, eyes narrowed with hatred and determination.

"Put your belt on," Kate shouted.

Tom scrabbled for his seat belt. The fastener clicked home just as Kate steered them into the back of another car. There was the hollow smack of metal on metal, and the 'wolf's muscular body was jolted clear. Its nightmare form slithered away into the darkness.

Kate shrugged as she slammed the car back into reverse. "Car's screwed anyway."

"So's my neck," said Tom, rubbing the back of it. "Can we stop playing keep-away now?"

"I guess so," Kate replied as they accelerated. "I don't think any of his friends are going to ask for a ride, do you?" she added mildly.

Tom shuddered and looked out at the lights that

were flickering on at most of the windows along the street. Warm little squares that spoke of cozy normality.

With the likes of Patience Stern living in their midst.

"I thought it was traditional for the wolf to eat the grandmother, not for the grandmother to eat every poor bastard who comes to visit. Though I guess she might have lost her appetite for a while." A flash frame of her broken body spliced itself into Tom's mind, and he shuddered. "She said Marcie had 'put out the word.' There'll be others after us, won't there?"

Kate nodded, hung a left. "You can bet on it. She'll have posted our descriptions on all the news-groups, mailed all her special contacts. . . ."

"Newsgroups?" Tom echoed. "Werewolves on the Web?"

"It's just like any other society, Tom," Kate replied, "only a lot more secret and a lot less harm-less. You might have noticed: werewolves don't all skulk around in Frankenstein's castle or misty grave-yards. They're everywhere, okay? Everywhere." She cut across two lanes to reach an exit, ignoring swerving cars and blaring horns. "And they were using the Web and e-mail years before there was a PC in almost every home. Reaching out to each other. Sharing information. Uniting, organizing."

"Okay, Kate, how about we slow down a little,

huh?" Tom suggested over the rising whine of the engine. "We don't want the cops pulling us over for speeding right now."

"The lupine community has never been stronger, Tom," Kate said, gripping the wheel so hard her knuckles showed white. "And now they're after us. There is no one, *no one* we can trust right now, okay? They want to kill us. You got that?"

"I got it!" Tom yelled at her. "I got it, okay, now will you stop the goddamned car before *you* kill us first?"

Kate braked hard and pulled over to the side of the road. The car lurched giddily as one wheel mounted the sidewalk beside a streetlight. The orange glow drowned out the sickly silver of the moonlight. She killed the engine. The cooling metal ticked noisily, like a bomb waiting to go off.

Tom sat for a while, waiting for her to speak. When she didn't, he sucked in a deep breath. "Where'd you go, Kate?" he asked.

Kate kept on staring out at the quiet highway.

"When I woke up, you were gone. And so was your backpack—with all the money."

"It's on the backseat," Kate replied.

Tom saw that her eyes were brimming with tears. He swallowed. "You ran out on me, didn't you?"

She shrugged, then nodded.

"What's the matter, my snoring that bad?"

"Yep." Kate gave a small smile. "You mad at me?"

"Mad at you?" Tom looked at her. "Sure. But more than anything, I'm hurt that you'd just leave without saying a word."

"I left a note," Kate muttered.

*A note—yeah, right.* "I didn't get it."

"I tucked it in your—"

Suddenly he couldn't hold it together any longer. "I don't care about some stupid note!" he yelled. "Writing doesn't count, okay? I'm not just a few lines of text in a chat room, winking and smiley-facing you from a gazillion miles away. I'm right *here*. I know it's not what you're used to but . . ." His voice dried, and he hoped Kate wouldn't see he was close to tears as well. "Look. I just need to know . . . that you won't run out on me again."

Kate's hands slipped from the wheel and fell into her lap. "I came back for you, didn't I?" she said quietly.

"Because of me? Or because of the 'wolves outside?"

She turned to face him, the look on her tearstained face darkening.

"Semicolon-dash–right parenthesis," he added, and mimed the emoticon for her.

When she smiled, he wished he could lean in to hold her and to be held. *In your dreams*, he told himself. *Not while you're stuck in your nightmares.*

Kate turned the ignition and the battered Chevy

rattled into new life.

"Know where we're going?" asked Tom.

"Not really," she admitted, calmer now. "But I guess at least now we know where we're coming from."

An hour later on the interstate it seemed that Kate had worked out a fair idea of where they were headed.

Twin Falls, Idaho. Her old home.

"Won't your mom be expecting us to head there?" Tom worried. "It's the same route the bus was taking."

Kate nodded. "But we need a new vehicle."

Tom looked at her quizzically.

"Think about it," Kate continued. "Someone drove into sweet old lady Patience's house—and her Chevy is missing. The cops are probably already looking for it. I'm hoping we can borrow something else from someone I know in Twin Falls."

"You said we can't trust anyone," Tom reminded her.

"This is different."

"You must know them pretty well."

Kate didn't answer.

Rocky stretches of desert and wilderness gradually gave way to wide-open fields. They arrived in Twin Falls as dawn was smudging trails of golden red across the paling sky. They drove past fields and farmhouses on the outskirts of town for a few miles, then Kate jerked hard on the wheel.

"Hey!" Tom cried as the Chevy started plowing a ragged swathe through a wheat field.

"Off-road and out of sight," Kate explained. She turned off the engine and the car slowed to a graceless halt. The wheat waved wildly in a stiff breeze, as if in surrender.

"Thanks, Patience," said Tom reverently. "Your car was a virtue even if you turned out not to be."

Kate didn't smile. She picked up her backpack, got out of the car, and walked away without looking back.

Tom followed her onto the road, where they walked for about a quarter of a mile before hitting a dirt path.

"This is the place," Kate told him.

The path swerved around a blind curve.

"So, who's this person you think can help us?" Tom asked.

Kate suddenly stopped dead in her tracks. "Him," she said.

Tom froze too. A blond-haired guy, probably in his early twenties, with clear blue eyes and a straggly goatee was standing in the middle of the path. He wore muddy jeans, a plaid shirt, and a heavy, waterproof jacket.

And he was pointing a shotgun at them.

## CHAPTER ELEVEN

"Hey, Jed," Kate said, pushing her hands deep into her coat pockets. "You going to shoot me or what?"

Jed was staring at her like Tarzan seeing Jane for the first time: part wonder and desire, part fear. He lowered the shotgun hesitantly. "Katie? Jesus, is it really you?"

A tiny smile appeared on Kate's face. "Yeah. Really."

Jed shook his head, disbelief stretching his face somewhere between goofy smile and baleful frown. "Three years since you disappeared."

"Long story," Kate told him, but before she could manage another word, Jed grabbed her in a clumsy hug.

Tom felt a cold spark of jealousy kick through him. Kate was embracing Jed too, her hands pressing against different parts of his back like she couldn't work out where best to hold him first. "Hi, I'm Tom Anderson," he announced loudly.

The two broke off the hug. Jed skittered back a few steps like he'd been sleepwalking and now he'd woken up with a shock. He nodded at Tom without enthusiasm. "Jed Monterey."

"Tom's a friend of mine," Kate said casually.

"Is that a fact?" Jed remarked.

"So, do you greet all your visitors at gunpoint?" Tom inquired.

"Saw you dump the car on our land," replied Jed. "Thought you might mean trouble." He turned back to Kate, and there was something raw in the way he looked at her. "Then I saw it was you, and—"

"Right the first time," she said stiffly. "We do mean trouble."

Jed looked quickly at Tom. Then he shrugged. "You want to come up to the house?"

"If that's okay," Kate said.

A keen wind was whipping up as they traipsed along the path to the farmhouse. Storm clouds were blowing in from the west, but the sun was still blazing in the early-morning sky. The few fall leaves dotting the bare branches glowed copper against the dark edges of cloud. Tom tagged along after Kate and Jed, feeling like a kid who couldn't quite grasp the undertones between the adults leading him on.

The farmhouse was old, its whitewashed exterior peeling and cracked. The heavy timber door stuck in its frame when Jed went to open it. He gave it a sharp kick. It loosened and he stepped through.

"I hope we won't be disturbing your folks," Tom said.

"They're farmers, Tom," said Kate, rolling her eyes. "Jed's dad gets up before he's even gone to bed."

"You being funny, Kate?" Jed asked hoarsely. It was like shutters had come down behind his eyes. "You know Dad's dead?"

Ouch. Tom felt his toes curl.

"No. I—I had no idea." Kate's face drained of color and she gripped hold of a kitchen chair. "I'm so sorry. When did—?"

"The night you left." Jed stared at her, his gaze glassy and unfocused. "Some kind of wild animal, police said, same kind as killed all the others. Slit him open from top to bottom."

Tom froze.

"I . . ." Kate put her hand to her chest, like she couldn't breathe.

Tom pulled out a chair for her to sit on. Its legs creaked across the stone floor like massive claws tearing the silence. He frowned at Jed. "Can we get her a glass of water?"

Jed nodded toward the sink. "There's a glass in the cupboard."

While Tom poured her the water, Jed leaned back against the kitchen counter. "It's my farm now. I run it for Mom. She hasn't been well since Dad died." He smiled, like he was mocking some childish dream. "Never did make it out of Twin Falls the way you did, Katie."

Kate shook her head as Tom tried to put the glass of water to her lips. "Where is your mom?"

"Over at Rodman's." Jed looked at Tom. "Rod's my brother. Owns a bigger farm the other side of town. Dad'd be real proud of him—he's done real well." That mocking smile again. "Me, I'm a better vet than I am a farmer. But I get by."

"You stay here alone?" Tom asked.

"Depends what you mean," said Jed, his eyes fixed on Kate like she'd asked the question. "Sometimes I think Dad's still here, watching over me. That's why I can't leave, can't sell up. Not till Mom—" He broke off, sighed heavily. "It'd break her heart to see all Dad's work die the way he did."

"I'm sorry." Kate appeared to be in a state of shock. "So sorry."

Jed shrugged. "It was three years ago. We never got over it. But maybe someday." He pulled up a chair and sat facing Kate. He placed his hand on hers. "With a little help, maybe someday."

Tom watched sulkily as Kate placed her free hand on top of his. He felt like the invisible man.

"It's kind of strange when the past comes running back and slaps you in the face," Jed went on, softly shaking his head. "Hey, you still got the scarf I gave you?"

Kate seemed to wake from a trance. "Uh . . ." She flushed. "The green one?"

"Uh-huh. It matched your pretty eyes."

"I . . ." A blush warmed Kate's pale complexion. "Uh, sure I do."

Jed nodded, apparently satisfied. "So, what's this trouble you mentioned?"

Kate's voice was flat, emotionless. "We need to dump the Chevy. Get new wheels. I can't tell you details."

Jed looked at Tom, a hint of menace in his glacial eyes. "Maybe *he* can."

"No." Kate shook her head. "Look, some people are coming after us. It's not safe for us to stay here too long—"

Jed snorted. "Running away again, Katie?"

"I didn't want to involve you, but there was no one else I could . . . trust." She squeezed his hand more tightly. "Jed, you have to trust me. Please, will you trust me?"

"I used to trust you, Katie," he whispered. "Where you running to now?"

"It's best you don't know," she replied.

"Best for me or best for you?" Jed retorted.

"For everyone."

Jed pulled his hand away. "Strange how you always know what's best for everyone without asking first."

"Uh, excuse me." Tom stood up suddenly.

"Obviously you two need to talk, so why don't I . . . ?"

Jed shook his head. "No. No, it's cool." He got up and grabbed his coat from its hook on the door. "Okay, I think I can get you a car. But I'll have to sort it out with Rodman first. Let me do that, and I'll be back around seven." He looked at Kate. "Rest here for the day, huh? The house is empty; no one'll disturb you."

Kate nodded and smiled wearily.

Jed slammed the door behind him. To Tom it felt like a cell door closing on him and Kate, shutting them inside.

"So your mom killed his dad," Tom said quietly.

"Figures. She hated me seeing him." Kate seemed lost in some private space. "Hated me dating a warm, kind human boy."

"Sweet." The word slipped bitterly out of Tom's mouth before he could catch it.

Kate ignored him, still away in her own world. "And I never knew. It *must* have been Mom. . . . She killed Jed's dad, wrecked his life, his whole family, just because she could. One last kill . . ."

A thought slid into Tom's mind. He looked at Kate. "So what happens if you mate with a . . . *warm, kind human* boy . . . instead of a werewolf?"

Kate turned to him slowly, a sneer on her face. "What are you trying to say? I was just fourteen, you sick jerk."

"Hey," Tom protested, "I wasn't saying you slept

with Jed. But *would* sleeping with someone . . . nor-mal . . . make any difference?"

Kate shrugged. "It might make it harder to turn me 'wolf later," she replied. "But ultimately . . ." She shook her head.

"So you and Jed really never . . . ?"

"What is your problem, Tom? Are you getting off on this?" Kate rose angrily, sending the chair crashing over behind her. Then tears filled her eyes. "You know, I really did think about sleeping with Jed. I tried really hard to fall in love with him so it would be okay. So I wouldn't just be using him. But even at fourteen I knew that if I cashed in my virginity to fend off the big bad 'wolf, then my mother had won. She would still have been dictating who I slept with, still control-ling me, and . . ." The tears were coming now in fat drops. "And you know, I like to think I'm worth more than that."

"You are," Tom told her quietly.

"And I like to think that I'm stronger than my fear of her and what she wants to do to me. . . ."

Tom reached out a hand to her, but she slapped it away.

"Go to hell," she hissed. She stormed from the kitchen.

Tom heard a distant door slam. Jed's bedroom door, maybe. How many times had the fourteen-year-old Kate fooled around with her older boyfriend in there? He shook his head. Why the hell was he getting so worked up over Kate? She could never want him. He'd been turned into the thing she hated most in the world. The thing that could destroy her. Tom felt the 'wolf shadow looming in the back of his mind, prickling his insides. If he could only go on fighting against it, show her that he really *was* a wereling or whatever her stupid old books told her he might be . . . Maybe then . . .

Tom kicked a chair clear across the room in frustration.

He stalked over to the kitchen phone, his mind dizzy with too many hurt and hurtful thoughts.

He dialed home. Listened to the intermittent purr of the ringing tone.

"Hello?"

His mother's voice. He opened his mouth to speak to her. The words stuck in his throat.

"Hello? Who's this?" She sounded tired, beaten down.

*Tell me everything will be okay, Mom,* he pleaded inside his head.

"Who *is* this?"

*I just don't know anymore.*

There was a rattling click as she hung up. Then the dial tone.

Tom walked out of the kitchen and found the living room next door. He sprawled out on the couch, too dazed and damaged even to cry. Birds were singing outside, blissfully unaware of the coming storm.

Sleep swept its own dark clouds over Tom.

"Wake up, Tom. Quick."

Tom stirred to find Kate crouched over him. Her hair was tangled and messed up. Her eyes, red rimmed and puffy, blazed at him urgently.

"What is it?" he snapped, a jolt of panic charging through him.

"People, outside." Kate grabbed his arm, pulled him up from the couch. He rubbed his eyes, stumbled over to the window, where a dusky sky touched with the last traces of sunset waited over the fields below.

Three dark figures in masks, holding blazing torches, were slowly closing in on the farmhouse.

## Chapter Twelve

"Jed?" Kate shouted, turning from the window. "Jed!"

Tom frowned. "He's not back yet, is he?"

"I thought—" Kate drew in a sharp breath. "I thought I heard the front door open."

Together they crept to the darkened kitchen and peered inside.

"Hey." Jed's voice sounded quietly out of the gloom, making them jump.

"Why are you hiding out here?" Tom asked sharply.

Kate asked no questions, just gripped Jed by the arms. "People are coming here for us. We've got to get out, and you've got to come with us."

"Me?" said Jed softly.

"You don't understand. They—they could kill you," Kate said, her body trembling with every breath. "Look."

She led him over to the window. The shadowy figures were getting closer. They were wearing dime-store Halloween masks—ghost, jack o'lantern,

Frankenstein's monster . . . the trick-or-treaters from hell. They paused to plant their flaming torches in the ground, then kept on coming.

"Damn right I don't understand," Jed muttered hoarsely. "All right. Down the hallway. We'll cut out through the front-room window."

Kate was nodding. "Into the woods?"

"That's right. We can lose them there." Jed stiffened. "But I've got to grab something first. C'mon, this way."

He led them quickly along the hallway and signaled them to stay put while he dashed upstairs, a shadow vanishing into blackness.

Tom was grateful for Kate's presence beside him as the taut seconds ticked by, their earlier quarrel forgotten.

"How did they find us so fast?" Tom muttered.

"I told you," said Kate dully. "They're everywhere."

Jed came slowly back down the stairs like he was afraid he might fall. His hands were hidden behind his back.

"Come on," Kate urged him.

"See this?" Something long and silky snaked out from Jed's balled-up fist. "You don't have that scarf I gave you. It's right here."

Kate stared at him, baffled. "Okay, I'm sorry, I guess I lost it. Now, can we—?"

"I found it, see," Jed said softly. "Lying by dad's body. Soaked in his blood."

Kate took a couple of faltering steps back, like Jed had just slapped her face. "What?"

Tom slipped a protective arm around her. "You can't believe Kate had anything to do with—"

"What the hell should I believe?" Jed yelled. "Dad was opened up like a fish for gutting. No wild animal did that to him, whatever the cops said." His voice quieted a little. "Your scarf was next to him. You feel like explaining that?"

"I had nothing to do with your dad's death, Jed," Kate said, her voice low and shaky. "You must believe that. And you must believe that we have to get out of here before those things outside—"

Tom heard the kitchen door being kicked open. He grabbed hold of Jed. "We have to go. *Now.*"

Jed punched him full in the face.

Kate gave a short shriek as Tom smashed back into the wall and slid down it, dazed.

The masked figures were charging down the hallway toward them. Stunned, Tom struggled to rise, felt Kate trying to pull him up by his arm, but it was too late. She was yanked away from his side by one of the intruders, and a second later he too was hauled to his feet.

"Who the hell is this creep?" came a gruff voice behind him.

"She's with him now," Jed explained. "Says they're in trouble. Someone's coming after them."

"Is that a fact?" the man said. "Well, whoever's chasing them will just have to wait in line."

Kate seemed to recognize the other guy's voice. "Rodman? Rod, is that you?"

"Got a good memory, don't you, Katie? Well, that's good. 'Cause so do we."

Tom watched in a daze as the man pulled off his Halloween mask. He looked like the archetypal astronaut, clean-cut and broad with a buzz cut, about thirty. "Yeah, it's me, Jed's big brother."

"Jeez, this is like an episode of *Scooby-Doo*. You'd have gotten away with it if it hadn't been for us meddling kids," muttered Tom, fighting to focus through the thick band of pain behind his eyes. "So are the rest of you going to take off your masks? I'm guessing it's the janitor, the butler—"

"They don't want to be identified, son," said Rodman with a cold smile. "In case things get a little out of hand."

He swung back around to face Kate, who was struggling in the grip of two thugs. "The police wrote off Dad's death as a wild animal attack. They weren't interested in answering any of my questions. Like why your family moved away so damn fast. Like why all the disappearances and killings in these parts stopped after you'd gone."

"I didn't kill your father!" Kate yelled at him.

"But you were involved, weren't you?" Rodman snarled. "Or else why was your scarf was found next to him?"

"I didn't tell anyone I'd found it," said Jed

quietly. "Didn't tell anyone till after the investigation."

"You were a damn fool," spat Rodman. "The cops didn't want to know then." He pressed his face up to Kate's. "I can smell it on you. Guilt." He laughed. "Well, I know all about guilt, Katie. Guilt is feeling we all let Dad down by settling for that bull-shit animal story instead of getting hold of the truth. Guilt is watching my ma going out of her mind with grief and knowing I can't do a damn thing to help." He grabbed Kate by her chin. "But now that we've gotten ahold of you, mystery girl, I reckon the truth's not far behind."

"What are we going to do?" asked Jed.

Rod laughed shortly. "Take them outside and I'll show you."

Tom and Kate were dragged helplessly out of the house and into the field outside. The long wet grass soaked their jeans.

Like oversized candles, the flaming torches planted outside glowed beckoningly. Their flickering light revealed a dark pile of sharp shadows that reached up higher than a man. Tom smelled the fierce tang of gasoline as he and Kate were shoved closer.

It was a pyre, piled high with sticks and tinder.

Someone was going to burn.

"No!" Kate shrieked, struggling harder. The men twisted her slender arms behind her back and she wailed in pain.

"Leave her alone!" Tom shouted, and was

smacked in the face by one of his captors. His lip stung and leaked blood. The taste made his guts tingle and churn.

"We're not really going to hurt her, though, right?" Jed was asking. "We're just going to scare the truth out of her, let the cops—"

"They'll do same as always. Zero," Rodman retorted. "It suits them to believe it was just some critter that killed Dad. And even if we forced her to admit to it, they'd only send her to a shrink." He shook his big head. "Truth is, you know what she's done. And you know what she *is*." He stepped up to Kate, his lips curling with remembered rage.

"It wasn't me," Kate spat at him.

"Tough when no one believes you, ain't it?" Rodman grabbed the green scarf from Jed and tied it around Kate's mouth, gagging her. "Like no one believed the folks swearing they'd seen a girl going into the woods and only a wolf coming out."

"I told you, Rod, that's crazy," Jed protested. But he didn't sound certain.

"Grab one of the torches," Rodman ordered; then he turned back to Kate. "The deaths stopped when you went away, *wolf girl*." Rodman gripped her cheeks with his thick fingers and squeezed. "So what'll it be? Show us the beast in you. I want to prove I was right all these years."

"It's not her you want, you idiot!" Tom yelled.

Rodman ignored him. "Show us!" he shouted.

"Or when I light the flames, you'll be howling soon enough."

Kate was trying to wriggle her face free of the gag, her eyes wide with fear.

"Jed, Rod's wrong! It's not true!" Tom roared. "You've got to believe us!"

"Take care of him," Rodman ordered, and Tom, struggling desperately, was hauled away into a ramshackle barn that stank of damp straw. The moon peeped in at him dispassionately through the gaping doorway.

"They're going to kill her," he yelled, more to the moon than the thugs pushing him around.

Frankenstein's monster kneed him in the stomach. Jack O'Lantern kicked him in the face. Tom fell backward and smashed into a wooden wall.

A pulse seemed to surge through his brain. Suddenly everything seemed to take on an extra degree of clarity. His senses tingled. It didn't matter that it was dark. He could smell his attackers' sweat and excitement, hear their knuckles crack as their hands became fists.

And outside he could hear Kate's muffled screams.

*"If you're sharp, you can bring on the change whenever,"* Wesley had said.

"Let me go," Tom croaked, on all fours. His bones were burning hot. His pores prickled with cold sweat. "You don't understand what you're doing."

139

"Awww, is he worried about his girlfriend?" jeered Frankenstein. The moonlight glinted on the brass knuckles he was pulling over his chunky fingers.

Tom staggered up and was knocked straight back down again. He cried out, a low, guttural sound.

Jack O'Lantern snickered. "She's pretty hot."

Tom heard the whoosh of the woodpile igniting into flame. The stifled screams grew more desperate.

"She's gonna get a lot hotter tonight."

A pressure filled Tom's head. He started to shake as a deadly, exhilarating purpose took hold of him. It shook him by the spine, squeezed his insides to pulp. The thugs no longer scared him. They made him hungry. His saliva pooled out in a puddle in front of him. He laughed uncontrollably as he saw his nails growing longer, saw wiry hairs worm their way out of his skin.

"Whoa. Look at him. Who *is* this freak?" breathed Jack O'Lantern.

Tom wondered how he'd borne being some nothing kid for so long when he had all this power, this potential inside him desperate for release. The changing was easier than last time. He rose up on all fours, shucking off the remnants of his human form and the clothes that covered it.

The men screamed, but not for long.

Step by step, Kate was being forced closer to the blazing pyre. The roaring flames seemed to reach out for her. The heat prickled her skin.

"Is this what it takes to make you howl for us?" screamed Rodman.

She threw back her head with all her strength. Her skull cracked against his nose and he yelped, loosened his grip. Kate yanked herself free, pulled the suffocating scarf clear of her mouth, gulped down lungfuls of smoky air.

"Stop her, Jed!" shouted Rodman, still sprawled out on the ground.

Jed moved to bar Kate's way out, then started to shake. She realized he was looking past her, his eyes widening in terror. Kate knew what she would see when she turned around.

The sleek, black-pelted werewolf was pounding toward them. It leapt through the flames of the pyre like it was emerging from hell, then landed in front of Rodman and let out a vicious growl.

Rodman started screaming like a terrified child.

"No, Tom!" Kate yelled.

But the creature Tom had become moved faster than words. It pounced on Rodman, placed a massive paw on his throat, cut off his screams.

"Don't do it," Kate pleaded with the slavering creature. "The 'wolves took his father, but you're not *like* them, Tom. You're different, I know you are."

The werewolf raised its heavy head toward her. She saw the eyes, brown and sad, staring out at her. Tom's eyes. But the creature wouldn't take its heavy paw from Rodman's throat.

Kate held her breath as seconds dragged by.

Finally the werewolf backed off. With a glance in her direction it fled, vanishing out of sight behind the fire.

"Tom, wait!" she yelled into the night.

"Rodman was right about the 'wolves," Jed breathed shakily.

"But he was wrong about me," Kate told him.

Jed nodded. His face was streaked with tears as he lifted the scarf from around her neck.

"I saved your brother's life," Kate said quietly. "Now help us like you promised and I'll get out of your life forever."

But Rodman had scrambled back to his feet. "Don't listen to her, you idiot," he said, his voice reedy, red welts rising on his throat. "We've got to make her talk—"

Jed hit him hard on the chin. Rodman went down and stayed down.

"I hope to God I'm doing the right thing," Jed said in a low voice.

Kate stayed silent. She could've blurted that it was Marcie who'd slaughtered his dad. That it was Marcie who'd left Kate's scarf by the body; maybe to trick him, maybe just warn him off her, to make sure he stayed well away or else risk the same fate. But what good would that do? Jed or his brother might set their sights on getting back at Marcie—and unlike Tom, she'd show them no mercy. The killing would go on.

Jed looked at the scarf. "I don't know how this got here . . . don't know how you're even involved. And I don't want to know. I already know more than I ever wanted to."

She watched as he wadded up the scarf and hurled it into the heart of the fire. There went Katie Folan. There went the past. Smoke blew in Kate's eyes, stinging them nearly to tears.

*I never liked that damn scarf anyway,* she told herself.

In the darkness beyond, a low, mournful howl rang out.

"So you need a car," Jed said. He handed her a key ring. "Take my pickup."

Kate nodded. "Thanks. I'll call you later and tell you where you can find it."

"Don't bother," Jed said quickly. "Been saving for a new one anyway."

Kate swallowed hard. She could see it in his stance, in the way he avoided her eyes—he could hardly stand to be around her now. He just wanted her gone, wanted no part of the nightmare that was her life.

"Thanks," she said at last. "Take care, Jed. I mean it."

He nodded, already backing away.

Kate walked slowly toward the barn Tom had been dragged to. She uprooted one of the flaming torches to light her way, dreading what she might see.

The two thugs lay sprawled in the wet straw. The

man in the Jack O'Lantern mask was unconscious, his chest a bloody crisscross of deep scratches. The other was whimpering softly to himself, clutching his sides, in deep shock.

She'd been right about the balance in him. Tom wouldn't kill, and neither would his 'wolf.

Planting the torch just outside for light, she went through their pockets and pulled out anything valuable or useful. She surveyed her haul. Forty dollars and some change. A watch with an expandable strap, a brass knuckles, and a skull ring. Well, it was something.

Tom's clothes lay in a heap. The shirt was shredded like the Hulk had been in town, but the jeans didn't look beyond repair. She quickly stripped the unresisting shaking guy to the waist and then removed his running shoes and leather belt.

Bundling up her spoils, Kate rose and crossed over to the boundary of the skeletal woods. Dead branches and leaves cracked beneath her feet like old bones. She sensed dark brown eyes watching her from the shadows, but boy or wolf, she couldn't be sure.

She laid the clothes and the watch down at her feet. The rest of the stuff she forced into her pockets.

"Don't catch a chill, wereling," Kate called into the trees. Her voice echoed through the branches. "Put these clothes on before they get soaked. There's a watch here too."

"Kate? You're okay?" Tom's voice carried clearly to her from the darkness.

"Thanks to you," she replied.

"Guess it was my turn for the rescue bit." Tom exhaled heavily. "I . . . let the 'wolf go. It was so hard to keep control."

Kate shivered in a sudden gust of wind. "Get dressed; we've got to go. Cross through the trees to the northwest and you'll come to a footpath. Turn right. It leads to the main road. I'll wait for you."

"Don't you want me with you?"

"I need a couple of moments alone right now. Okay?"

Tom didn't answer. But as she turned away, Kate heard him lope over for the clothes before returning to the cover of the forest.

Kate walked to the pickup, got inside, and closed the door. Turned the key in the ignition.

She drove jerkily away, down the path and out onto the main road for a quarter of a mile. Then she parked at the top of the footpath she'd mentioned to Tom, switched off the headlights, and waited.

The landscape was dark beneath the sky's starry static. She checked the luminous face of her watch. It would be a few minutes yet before Tom got here. She was alone. Free to do as she wished. She should cherish this time.

Hugging herself, Kate rested her forehead on the cold plastic of the steering wheel and sobbed.

## CHAPTER THIRTEEN

Kate and Tom passed most of the four-hundred-mile journey in silence, each lost in their thoughts. But it was a comfortable silence. They drove through the night to reach Salt Lake City as soon as possible.

"We can pick up an Amtrak train there, and also the library has free Internet access," Kate explained. "We went on a field trip to Salt Lake when I was twelve. Had to look up our family trees."

"Oh yeah, the Mormon Family History Library, right?" Tom replied. "I read about that. Has practically every family in America in it." He frowned. "But *your* kind of family isn't logged there, surely?"

"Uh-huh. Under *w* for *werewolf*," Kate deadpanned. She reached out and slapped the side of his head lightly. "Stupid. Birth registrars don't screen for freaks of nature. There's nothing to mark out my family as any different from yours. And I traced my family name back to sixteen-oh-something."

Tom nodded. "Purebloods, of course. Nice clear family line."

"We were known as Phelans back then. My ancestors came over from Europe."

"I kind of wish they'd stayed there," said Tom. "Remind me why we want free Internet access again?"

Kate glanced at him. "So I can e-mail my contacts and get them busy. See if we can find a warm trail to our medicine man Jicaque when we hit New Orleans."

"I guess he's not likely to be in the phone book." Tom sighed.

"It's rumored he's retired," she confessed. "He was pissing off too many 'wolves, so they gave him an ultimatum: Stop and you can live."

"Terrific." Tom scowled. "So even if we find him, he's not going to risk his life for my sake, is he?"

"I told you, werelings are rare. You'll arouse his professional interest." She shot him a glance. "Besides, who could resist you, huh?"

"Funny." Tom snorted and turned away to hide his flushing cheeks. He didn't speak for the rest of the journey, staring out of the window as the Wasatch Range grew larger and turning Kate's compliment (was that what it was?) over and over in his mind.

Kate sent a myriad of e-mails from the library while Tom bought Amtrak tickets.

"We can't get there sooner than Thursday," Tom

told Kate once they'd met back up outside the Mormon Tabernacle. "The next train to Chicago doesn't leave till four in the morning, so we won't get there till late Wednesday afternoon. Then the connecting train to New Orleans leaves at 8 p.m., getting us in at about four in the afternoon the next day."

"Did you swallow that schedule?" Kate chewed her lip. "Jeez, this is going to be a long day. Still, hopefully by then we'll have some leads to follow up when we arrive."

"How do you know we can trust any of these contacts of yours?" Tom asked worriedly.

"They've been my friends for three years," said Kate.

"But you never met them!"

"Mom and Dad don't know about them. I wiped my Net cache each time I logged off; I have about a squillion e-mail addresses—"

"Okay, okay!" Tom sighed. "Guess I'm just paranoid."

"I can't imagine why." Kate smiled.

They passed the time drifting in and out of coffee bars, and when everything closed up, they laid low in a mission hall, living it up on free pea soup.

The train pulled away on time at 4 a.m. They had a sleeper compartment, small but clean.

Tom sat experimentally on the bottom bunk.

"Me and my brother had bunk beds when we were younger," he said. "Joe always whined till I let him take the top."

"So you'll let me have it without a fight. Excellent." Kate swung her lithe body up onto the top bunk with little difficulty. She bounced around a bit.

Tom lay back and pushed his feet against the underside of her bed, rocking it. Kate yelped and hung her head over the edge to frown at him.

They held each other's gaze for a few seconds. Long enough for it to maybe mean something. Tom's stomach muscles tightened.

Then Kate bobbed back out of sight. "I can't imagine what it's like," she said quietly, "having a brother you love. A brother who doesn't want you dead."

Tom drew in a deep breath, willing the heat in his skin to dissipate. "We threatened to kill each other enough times, believe me," he replied. "All this is probably some kind of punishment for taking my whole family so much for granted."

"Probably," Kate agreed, "you gloomy bastard." She paused, suddenly serious again. "My punishment's still waiting for me."

"You don't think being on the road with me is punishment enough?" he ventured.

"Of course I do," said Kate swiftly. "But I doubt if my dear mother will see it that way."

The train raced on along the tracks, keeping pace with Tom's heartbeat at the thought of Kate stretched out above. His bunk was narrow, but he wished Kate was sharing it with him.

With a sudden chill, he imagined Marcie Folan would just love that.

He had never spent this much time alone with a girl in his life. And maybe he was feeling the way he did because he was scared, lonely, and vulnerable— and admittedly, because he was sixteen, and lusting after good-looking girls came with the territory— but that didn't make the situation any less real. Maybe chasing him and Kate cross-country, driving them together, making them more and more dependent on each other was part of Marcie's plan. Because if by some miracle there ever *could* be something between him and Kate, that would be it: the Folans, the 'wolves, would win.

Unless they could find Jicaque. Unless Jicaque could heal him and drive out the 'wolf. Kate had told him that if she slept with someone human, it might make her less susceptible to . . .

He reined in his thoughts. Was that how he'd put it to her? "Let's do it—it would boost your immunity and give me a hell of a rush, whaddaya say?"

He had to smile despite himself. Above him he could hear Kate pulling off her sweater and wriggling out of her jeans, oblivious to his fevered thoughts.

Or maybe lost in a few of her own?

She yawned noisily. "Never mind werewolves.

All this sleeping all day and staying awake all night—we're becoming vampires."

"Not me," Tom whispered. "Once bitten, twice shy."

In the cramped little sleeper, listening to Kate's rhythmic breathing, Tom felt safer than he had for days. Sleep came easily.

But then the old nightmare of the dark beast with yellow eyes that ran like the wind returned. Tom's only comfort on jolting awake, slimy with sweat, was that the beast had been chasing after him and Kate together. Together.

The journey passed. They changed at Chicago, and Tom had wished he could change his clothes too. His split jeans weren't exactly ideal gear for keeping out the cold September rain as they killed five hours in the windy city. Their sleeper compartment on the new train was identical to the last one, but this time Kate took the lower bunk. Not that it helped. Tom spent hours trying not to imagine scenarios in which he "just happened" to roll off his bunk and accidentally land in hers. . . .

He tried reading Kate's dusty werewolf book to pass the time, but it was all too depressing. Instead he flicked through the guide to New Orleans they'd picked up from a Barnes & Noble in Chicago, trying to file away some local knowledge for when they arrived. His concentration was severely affected by Kate's bra, sticking out from a pile of her discarded clothes. It wasn't lacy or anything, just a plain chewing-gum-gray cotton. But the damned thing seemed to be magnetizing his eyes.

He checked the watch Kate had given him for about the zillionth time and realized with relief that within the hour they would reach their destination.

They were going to make it.

"Fifty minutes!" Tom called.

Kate gave an ironic whoop of joy and began dressing again on the bunk. Tom caught a sweet trace of her scent and breathed in discreetly to taste a little more.

"Are you trying to smell me, you perv?" she demanded.

*Ouch.* "I bet they can smell you in the next compartment," he covered languidly. "You stink. Go take a shower."

"That's a plan."

Tom bade a mental farewell to her bra as it was grabbed from the pile and waved a real one to the fully dressed Kate shortly after as she vanished off to the bathroom in the next car to freshen up.

When she didn't return within fifteen minutes, he was puzzled.

By the time twenty minutes had gone by, he was getting worried.

Tom was about to go looking for her when someone tapped loudly on the door. "Who's there?" he asked uneasily.

"It's the porter, sir," said a Midwestern-sounding voice. "I have a message from your friend."

Tom threw open the door. A freckle-faced man in his twenties, his long blond hair stuffed up in a peaked cap, nodded in greeting.

"What's wrong?" Tom asked.

"Your girlfriend has been taken ill, sir." The porter looked grave. "She's in the restaurant car, along there."

"She's not my—" Tom broke off and frowned. "But she went to use the bathroom. What's wrong with her?"

The porter shook his head worriedly. "I wish we knew, sir."

They hurried along the passageway. Tom noticed a red nick on the porter's cheek where he'd cut himself shaving. The blood didn't look long dried. Maybe he'd just come on shift, in a hurry. Which could also explain why his shirt wasn't tucked properly into his trousers. But how come the trousers were a good inch too short for him . . . ?

With a sinking feeling, Tom knew this had to be a trap.

They reached the restaurant car. The door was closed, a curtain over the window.

The porter was now blocking his way back, a patina of sweat on his face. "Quick, sir. She's been calling for you."

Tom hesitated. What choice did he have? He had to know what had happened to Kate.

He pushed open the door.

To his relief, the car was half filled with ordinary diners, Mr. and Mrs. Average chatting and laughing as they shoveled down steaks and fries. And he could almost *feel* Kate, somewhere close by.

"Look at the back of the car, sir," whispered the porter discreetly.

Tom could see someone under a blanket on the banquette at the far table—that must be her. He made his way there, still uneasy, glad that the porter wasn't following.

The figure on the banquette was completely covered by the blanket. It wasn't Kate. He could tell that from here. It was too short, lacked any real form. It was obviously just a couple of pillows or something.

He dropped to one knee, pretending to tie his shoelace to buy some time. Beside him were two businesswomen, dining together in sleek suits.

"That porter's a fake," he whispered to them. "I think he might've hurt my friend. Please, if I string him along, can you get some help?"

The women stopped eating. They looked first at him, then dubiously at each other.

"I think he stole his uniform—look at it!" Tom hissed. "If I'm wrong, then it won't matter, but . . . *please,* get someone."

"I'll go, Mary," said the older of the two, raising her eyebrows.

"Don't be long, Jan," whispered her friend with a nervous look at Tom.

The older woman got up and left the car. Tom rose to his feet with a sigh of relief. He looked again at the lumpy body bundled on the seats. "Is this some kind of joke?" he called to the porter.

"Goodness, no, sir," the porter replied innocently.

Tom yanked back the blanket. "Oh, come on, it's obviously just a . . ." His voice died away in a dry retch.

It wasn't a pile of pillows. The body under the blanket was real enough.

It was just in pieces.

Tom saw a blood-smeared railroad photo ID on a chain. This must be the real porter. He threw the blanket back over the bloodied mess, his other hand clamped over his mouth.

"Anything wrong, sir?" the fake porter called. "I'm here to help."

"You killed this man," Tom accused.

"Killed him?" Mary jumped up from her table in terror, backed away from the porter, and clutched Tom for support.

The fake porter looked at Tom, his eyes wide. "I most certainly did not, sir," he said. Then he smiled and pointed at Mary. "She did."

Mary's horrified expression changed into a smirk

as she sank her long fingernails into the flesh of Tom's arm. "He's right," she said softly. A gleam of yellow spun through her eyes.

"Help me!" Tom shouted at the other diners, his arm burning with pain. They looked uncertainly at each other, as if all this might be some big joke.

Tom tore his arm free of Mary's grip and ran for the door. But Mary's friend Jan stepped through it and blocked his way.

"I'm sorry," Jan said with a grin. "The staff seem to be . . . indisposed." She held a knife in her hand. Both blade and handle were sticky with blood.

Tom backed up against Mary. She licked her lips.

The fake porter took a step toward him. "See . . . if I deliver you and the girl to Papa Takapa, I'll have proved myself worthy."

Tom stared at him. "Papa who?"

"Papa Takapa," the man repeated, his voice reverent. "If I please him, he will turn me *himself*."

"And you actually want that?" Tom asked him, disbelieving.

"Why shouldn't we?" Jan demanded. "He's promised me too," she added in the same worshipful tone. "As humans we serve him, and when we become 'wolves, we will share in his power. His bite will place us above the rank and file. It's his blessing."

"No. No, it's not!" Tom stared wildly around at the other passengers. There were eight or nine of them, just staring. "Please, won't *any* of you help me?"

"Depends what kind of help you want, sweet lips," murmured Mary.

The diners began to twitch and shake. Tom stared around in horror as the air was suddenly filled with the cracking of bones, hoarse whimpers, low, threatening growls.

They were 'wolves. All of them.

The porter moved toward him, entranced as all around him sickly yellow eyes rolled wildly in their sockets, clothes ripped open and tore free. Skin stretched like rubber over protruding jaws, and lengthening, strengthening limbs sprouted thick hair all over.

"I don't think that meal was quite to my friends' liking," whispered Mary as her features began to shift and blur too. "They're still hungry."

## CHAPTER FOURTEEN

Tom's mind raced through possible courses of action. He could try to bring on his own change, pit 'wolf against 'wolf. But what chance would he stand against an entire pack of lupines?

Before him, Mary opened her jaws and laughed, perhaps hoping to scare him with the horror of her transformation.

But Tom was getting used to horror. He pushed her aside and turned back to the porter. "You really want to join the ranks of these freaks? Here!" He kicked the man in the groin as hard as he could.

With a groan of agony the porter fell back into the laps of two 'wolves who were in mid-change. Instinct kicked in and, ignoring his protesting shrieks, they bit and tore at him.

"Don't forget to write," Tom muttered.

He turned back to the door. Jan, still blocking his way, slashed at his face with the knife. He dodged aside, and she sliced into her friend's arm instead.

The creature—what was left of Mary's human

form, doubly macabre in the tattered remains of the business suit—howled in pain as blood spurted out of the wound. Reflexively she slashed at her friend's face with her club-like paw. The woman collapsed onto a table, wiping frantically at her eyes, spitting blood from her mouth, unable to see Mary's wide jaws closing on her whole head.

Tom turned away, lunged for the door. The sound of flesh tearing made a part of him sick and another part salivate. He wanted to join them, to feed on warm flesh. And he hated himself for it.

But it wasn't just him. The smell of so much blood in the small restaurant car was driving the transforming werewolves into a frenzy. One of them clawed at Mary's chest, another at her leg, then another until she keeled over.

The fake porter's long blond hair had come free of his cap and now spilled over his face, hiding his wounds from view. "It's him you want!" he gasped, trampled beneath the heavy beasts as they milled about in the confined space. "The boy! Get the boy!"

Tom hit the open button on the door, which slid lazily aside. He shot through and prayed it would close again swiftly. Tom guessed that Papa Takapa, whoever he was, wanted him alive—but he knew from hideous personal experience how powerful the urge for blood was. If the 'wolves fell upon him with that lust unsatisfied, he might end up being delivered in pieces.

Fortunately for him the 'wolves were still in disarray, snapping and snarling. Feasting. Tom ran down the corridor to the next compartment, an empty kitchen area. A man lay slumped in a corner, blood pooling from a wound in his chest. Grimly Tom dragged the corpse into plain view in the passageway, muttering apologies under his breath. Maybe the corpse would distract the 'wolves for a while.

Through the window he saw the world outside blurring by at easily eighty miles an hour. There was no way out here. And no Kate.

He swore. Where had she been taken? Logic told him that Marcie would want to keep her daughter alive. After all, with Wesley dead, it was down to Kate to carry on the pureblood Folan name. But would this Takapa dude feel the same way?

There was a crash from the restaurant car down the corridor. He didn't have long.

A fire extinguisher on the wall was rattling in its housing as the train sped along. He smashed it against the window as hard as he could. By the fourth blow a crack appeared, and by the seventh he had knocked a hole in it. Wind whistled inside the car harder and faster as he smashed out the rest of the glass.

Tom stuck his head out of the window, his hair whipping against his forehead. Fear formed a tight block in his stomach. He couldn't swing himself out the window and expect to hold on, going at that speed. It was a crazy idea.

Tom heard the door in the restaurant car sigh gently open.

On the other hand, it was the only idea—and the only chance—he had.

He stuck his head out through the window again, squinting into the wind. There were corrugated ridges in the gray metal of the car, above and below the window, just enough to give him something to cling on to.

Now or never.

Tom hauled himself out through the window. For a few seconds he balanced on its sill. The world seemed to be going by at a million miles per hour. He turned, still gripping the sill, and placed his feet in one of the ridges. Then, first with one hand, then with the other, he gripped the ridge above the window.

Now the challenge was to redistribute his weight and shuffle toward the engineer's car while trying to stay as flat to the side of the speeding train as possible. The wind pulled at his clothes, threatened to tug him away like a straw doll in a gale. Clinging for his life, he edged along the rocking car. Already his fingers were losing feeling.

A metal ladder stretched up to the train roof at the end of the compartment. It was just a few yards away. . . .

A terrifying, ululating howl rose above the keening of the wind in his ears. Turning his head, he saw the massive head of a werewolf poking through the window. Another one pushed into view beside it, scenting the air until it turned to face him. Yellow eyes narrowed; fangs bared.

Raw fear pumped renewed strength through Tom's body. He clawed his way along the ridges in the train's side with greater speed.

But the first werewolf had decided to follow him.

Tom glimpsed the monster from the corner of his eye as it twisted in the window frame and reached out tentatively to test the ribbed surface of the car walls. And suddenly he remembered the beast that had clung onto the hood of Patience's car back in Caldwell.

Sure enough, like an animal mountaineer using claws instead of crampons, the man-wolf began to scale the side of the car. It swung its bulk from paw to paw, stalking Tom, leaving a trail of ripped metal in its wake.

It would reach him before he could reach the ladder.

Gritting his teeth, he tried to move faster. The ground rushed by below him, an unending blur of movement. He felt sick, his heart pounding with exertion and terror. And in a black, burning part of his mind he knew his desperation was giving strength to the rising urge to let go of his humanity, to give rein to the 'wolf. To turn fear into fury and to wash clean the bitter taste of panic from his mouth with blood.

Then he saw the tunnel.

He glanced back at the werewolf, lurching ever closer with sinister, crab-like movements. Its eyes were narrowed against the wind, its dagger teeth bared and ready to tear at him. It was so much bigger than he was.

The maw of the tunnel seemed to open wider as the train thundered toward it. Tom pressed himself flat against the chilled metal of the car.

The werewolf roared in triumph and readied itself for a final lunge. Tom shut his eyes.

There was a sickening, splintering noise as the beast's bulk was pulverized against the concrete; then the air turned to steam and blackness. Tom was nearly plucked free and dashed against invisible walls as the train rushed heedlessly on.

But when it emerged on the other side, so did he.

With the last of his energy he reached out for the arms of the ladder. He relished the feel of curling his fingers around rungs after trying to dig his fingertips into the solid metal. He could hold on now to the ladder and to himself, numb, desensitized by the stinging wind. The 'wolves knew he was out there, but none seemed willing to pursue him further any longer.

Tom wasn't sure how long he clung on there, but a terrible baying from inside the compartment roused him with a start.

The train was starting to slow down, ready to

pull into the station. Tom assumed that the 'wolves would turn human again, change into fresh clothes, and melt into the crowds.

He was wrong. One by one they leapt from the broken train window and hit the ground running. Now they seemed almost like actual wolves, as if the transformation had progressed still further; they'd pretty much lost the man form altogether. Moving as one, the pack veered away from the tracks and sprinted across the outskirts of the station yard for the protection of the storage buildings.

Tom knew he must hit the ground running too. He had to get away before someone discovered the carnage in the restaurant car, before Kate was taken away to face God knew what.

*"My punishment's still waiting for me,"* she'd said.

Recklessly he scaled the ladder, slid across the roof, and dropped down between the restaurant car and the locomotive. As he crouched in the narrow space, no one standing on the platform seemed to notice him. But he knew 'wolf eyes must be watching the train keenly.

At last the train came to a complete halt. Tom wriggled between the car and the locomotive and jumped the gap between train and platform. His legs felt like mush as he ran back up the length of the train, looking in at every car window, searching for Kate. But there were too many people surging off onto the platform, barging past him, blocking his view.

"Clear the way, clear the way," yelled a paramedic fighting his way through the crowds with more success than Tom. He was running for the restaurant car as if trying to escape the rest of his team, who were following close behind, weighed down with medical supplies and emergency equipment.

Clearly someone had found the bodies. Tom only hoped Kate's wasn't among them.

Fighting back his anxiety, Tom decided to wait around the main station exit instead, where he might get a better view of who came out. But the way was blocked by a couple of officious cops, rudely clearing a wide area around the restaurant car, seemingly more to bait the crowds than to aid the paramedics.

They were bearing out bodies on stretchers. Struggling to push through the crowds of onlookers, Tom glimpsed the fake porter, his stolen uniform bathed in blood, as he was lifted clear by two men in green. He doubted that Papa Takapa, or whatever his name was, would be in a hurry to bestow the power of the wolf on that loser. Close behind the impostor, a glossy black body bag was hauled out by two more men. What was left of the real porter, maybe?

No.

He'd seen movement. The body bag was *wriggling*.

"Kate," Tom breathed.

He shoved his way through the crowd like a crazy man. "Get out of my way!" he yelled. "Let me through!"

A big man scowled. "Wait your turn like the rest of us, buddy."

"She's not dead!" Tom yelled. "The girl in that body bag, she's still alive, she's moving!"

But the paramedics were rushing her away.

He was going to lose her.

Heart pounding, Tom looked for a way through the impenetrable crowd. "Stop them!" he yelled, but he knew he sounded like a lunatic. It was the perfect disguise; who would ever stop medics carrying a corpse from a crime scene?

The 'wolves were reclaiming their own, and there was nothing he could do.

Not like this.

He sank his nails into his palms. The pain sent sparks up and down his spine. He almost laughed as the first tingles of the changing went through him.

*People could get hurt,* a part of him warned.

*Kate* could get hurt if he didn't. The risk was worth it. And his anguish was already receding as lupine blood pumped hungrily through his twisting veins.

*Kate's only an excuse. You want the change, need it. You're just a different kind of junkie and this is your fix.*

But the voice didn't matter. The crowds didn't matter. He had to reach Kate, had to bring her back. And if his puny human self couldn't cut it, then the 'wolf would.

His muscles turned to mush, then re-formed in harder, more powerful designs. His shirt split open as he hunched forward, and coarse dark hair started sprouting from every follicle. All around him people were panicking, scattering, screaming. He bounded like a true beast across the station concourse, consciousness dimming, straining to catch the faint, cold plastic scent of the body bag.

An ambulance was parked outside the station. Medics were loading up bodies.

Tom would give them some more to deal with.

## CHAPTER FIFTEEN

Kate flinched from the sudden light as the medic unzipped the body bag. She gratefully gulped fresh air until a hand clamped down over her mouth.

"You going to be a good girl and stay quiet?" A medic was standing over her with a syringe. "Or do I have to put you to sleep?"

Kate shook her head, and the man took his hand away. Glancing around, she guessed she was inside an ambulance. Specially hired for the occasion, she had no doubt. Whoever these people were, they were well organized.

The moment Kate had stepped out of the bathroom on the train, she'd had a rag with some kind of knockout stuff held over her nose and mouth. That was it, lights out. When she'd woken up, she thought she'd been buried—it was dark, cramped, and airless. But then the lid had lifted on her prison and she'd found herself stuffed inside one of the banquette seats in the restaurant car. She'd caught only a glimpse of the carnage in the car but enough to know that it looked like the Texas Chainsaw Massacre had jumped a state.

Was Tom among the bodies? No one would answer her as she was bundled into the body bag, zipped up, and hauled away with another casualty.

Now another medic jumped into the back of the ambulance, slammed the doors behind him, and banged hard on the driver's partition. "We've got company," he shouted. "Get out of here."

Kate craned her neck and saw, through the twin windows of the double doors, a sleek, muscular 'wolf bounding toward them. Its eyes were dark, and the tatters of its blue jeans were held in place by a tough leather belt. "Tom!" she screamed.

At the same moment she kicked out at the handle securing the double doors. As the ambulance pulled away, both doors swung open. The medic angrily hauled one back shut, but Tom leapt through the other, his mutated form framed in a rectangle of noise and daylight.

Kate could hear shrieks from pedestrians outside and car horns blaring as the ambulance swerved from side to side, trying to accelerate into the traffic.

The medic with the syringe jabbed it into the 'wolf's neck and sank the plunger down. The sinewy flesh convulsed as the drug went in. Tom roared with pain, and the medic went sprawling back as Tom's powerful claws caught him a glancing blow.

"Watch out, Tom!" Kate yelled.

The other medic had grabbed a fire extinguisher. He primed it and let out a blast of white smoke right in the werewolf's face.

Caught by surprise, Tom recoiled and lost his footing.

Kate gasped as Tom fell and rolled backward over and over across the road before crashing into some trash cans.

"Get us the hell out of here!" yelled the medic, yanking the doors closed again. "Before we have the cops on our tail as well as a damn wereling!"

Kate gasped. So she wasn't the only one to have guessed.

"Shame we couldn't have grabbed him too," said the other man, fishing around in a first-aid box for a Band-Aid to cover the cut on his forehead. "We better tell Takapa before it's all over the news channels. He'll want to hear a firsthand account of what went down here."

"Takapa?" Kate asked. "Who is Takapa?"

"Keep quiet," snarled the medic.

"I'm not scared of you," Kate informed him tartly. "So how about you just tell me what you injected that 'wolf with?"

"This," answered the other man. A needle scraped her skin, and a flood of cold entered her arm.

Someone switched the world off and Kate sank into blackness.

Tom scrabbled up from the roadside. He couldn't think straight. It was as if his thoughts were in a language he couldn't quite understand.

*Angry. Hunger.*

These were things that couldn't help Kate, but the memory of her was dimming now.

People were shouting and staring. The world was too bright. Tom scurried away down a side alley, searching for darkness, but his limbs were heavy and cold despite the mild day. It was the needle, the thing they'd pushed into his skin. He was slowing down.

Then he smelled meat. Hot steam was pouring from a vent housed in the wall, reeking of roasting flesh. He trailed thick saliva as he pushed a heavy plastic door open and snuffled into a noisy kitchen. Men in stained uniforms were throwing chunks of meat into sizzling oil or attending to carcasses with sharp knives.

Tom's eyes narrowed.

*Butcher. Hunger.*

He could "attend" to *them*.

*Kill. Tear.*

No. The word changed in his head.

*Tears.*

He backed away, knocked down a stack of metal

trays. They clanged and clattered like a dinner gong, but Tom knew he must stay hungry. If he gave in to the 'wolf's instincts now, he knew he might lose his own forever.

He hobbled away through a maze of side streets, wrestling with his emotions until time lost all meaning.

When he came to, he was shaking and sobbing, half naked in the remnants of the day's sunlight. His skin was pale and hairless, human again. His stomach ached for food, but his heart was sick for something else.

If he hadn't been drugged, lethargic, weak before he'd entered that kitchen . . . what might he have done?

Tom looked around fearfully and found he had crawled into the middle of a cemetery; a city of the dead populated with stones and crosses and moldering angels. Here he was, one more set of human remains. He wiped his tears with the back of his hand, his thoughts and deeds as 'wolf only half remembered, like the dead all about him.

As he lay gathering his strength, the sun sank lower and the shadow of a crumbling brick mausoleum began to creep over him. Tom shrank away from it and stood up. He had no shoes or socks, his torn jeans were now barely cutoff shorts, and his shirt had torn clear away—but he began to walk anyway. Right now he needed to be in the light.

It was a mild evening, a little humid. He threaded

between the overgrown graves and shadowy stones and out into the street beyond.

It was a run-down, drab area. Mournful notes faltered nervously out of a saxophone from somewhere high up in a shabby building. Kids from the housing projects, dressed in rags little better than his, watched him with big eyes as he walked past. Somehow he had to find Kate, but first he had to find his own bearings.

The architecture, the whole feel of the place, was like he'd stepped into another time, maybe a century ago. Joggers and dog walkers stared at him in his rags, some amused, some afraid. Creole speakers chatted in groups on the stoops of the tall buildings. Giving thanks that it had been a sunny day, he hunted about the stuccoed houses in side streets and soon found a laundry line in someone's backyard. Tom plucked a shirt, some khakis, and a pair of plaid boxers from the sagging nylon cord, like strange fruit from a branch. He had no money, so he pinned his borrowed watch to the line instead and hoped the payment would be acceptable.

Ducking back out of the yard, Tom scuttled off with his damp prizes. In the next street he found the back entrance to a ramshackle old movie theater. A faded sign proclaimed it to be the Cinema Medin. The fire door, a mess of torn and faded posters, was ajar. Needing a place to change out of sight, Tom ducked inside.

He found himself in a corridor that gave onto a cramped and dusty auditorium. Cobwebs shrouded the crimson drapes of moth-eaten velvet, and rats squeaked and scuffled as they played among the slashed seats.

Tom had just slipped on the khakis when he heard a man's voice, dried and reedy with age.

"Do you need assistance, my friend?"

Tom looked up in alarm and discerned a dark figure watching him from a seat in the back row.

"Where y'at, son?" the old man tried again.

"Is this your place?" Tom glanced around nervously, wondering who else might be watching. "I didn't break in or anything."

"That's okay." The old-timer rose stiffly from his seat. "It's the rats' place as much as mine, but they're not the best company. You doin' all right? Maybe I could help you."

"I'm sixteen years old," Tom told him, roughing up his voice a little in case Pops thought he could try something. "I can dress myself, thanks."

The man stepped forward, and in the chink of light let in by the open fire door, Tom saw that he had reddish skin, broad cheekbones, and long gray-streaked dark hair. He looked like some sort of Native American. He was dressed all in black. "Not that kind of help," the man said mysteriously.

"Sorry, man," Tom said, backing away. "But I didn't come here to give you a private show." He balled up the tatters of his old jeans. "Be seeing you, okay?"

"Yes, I think you will," said the old man, smiling grimly.

Tom turned and fled from the Cinema Medin, not stopping till he was a good two blocks away, but there was no sign that he was being followed.

Things could be better, he decided, as he slung the shredded remains of his old jeans into a nearby trash can. The old man had creeped him out big time. His bare feet stung from running along the cracked and grimy pavement, and the stolen shirt was cold and clammy, chafing his skin.

"The only werewolf in town with athlete's foot and jogger's nipple," Tom reflected ruefully.

A thought struck him. He pulled his old jeans back out from the trash and delved halfheartedly into the pockets, just in case he was carrying cash without even realizing it.

From a back pocket he pulled out a dog-eared piece of white paper, folded in four. Tingles chased themselves across his chest as he opened it and read:

*Sorry, sick boy.*

> *It's me they want most, and I need to pick up speed.*
>
> *Go on to New Orleans. AB@Bloodlettings.com can help find Jicaque. Troll Lover said so.*
>
> *Good luck from one who needs it too.*
>
> ☹
>
> K

Tom frowned, not comprehending what he was reading. Then it clicked: this was the note Kate had written him when she ran out on him back at Patience's house. He'd been carrying it around with him ever since.

He traced a finger over her spidery handwriting. It felt to him like the paper dated from a whole different era, even though it was only a few days old. Kate had seemed so distant back then. Distant as his old life seemed to him now.

Tom studied the note again. *Bloodlettings*. Didn't sound very enticing, but marginally preferable to a troll lover, whatever that was.

Anyway, it was all he had.

There was a discarded copy of yesterday's *Times-Picayune* by the trash cans. Tom leafed through the paper until he found an ad for a cybercafe. A passing couple gave him directions, and he set off on tender feet for the Arts District.

When Kate awoke, she found herself slumped in a chair in a chilly storeroom. A dim bulb glowed over her head. Rusting shelf units supported boxes and crates, all unmarked. A table had been placed in the middle of the room before her. She imagined someone unpleasant would be sitting behind it before long.

Something else with unpleasant possibilities sat just behind her: a black bucket, with a roll of toilet paper and some antiseptic wipes. She shuddered. Clearly someone would be keeping her here for some time.

Then again, maybe she'd wind up too numb even to notice; a low humming noise told her this place was refrigerated. The temperature couldn't be far above freezing. Someone had draped a blanket around her shoulders, and she supposed she should be grateful, but the gratitude left her the second she tried to stand. Her ankle was cuffed to the heavy chair she'd been dumped in, and she fell forward with a yelp of surprise.

The noise brought someone.

Kate heard bolts sliding back, looked up, forced a look of icy defiance onto her face. It slipped as soon as she saw who had come to visit.

"Well, well. Groveling on the floor where you belong?"

"Patience," Kate gasped.

The old woman rolled into the room, her bulk squeezed into an electric wheelchair. A fierce line of stitches puckered her brown skin from cheek to chin, and her eyes were bruised yellow-black. She kept one hand beneath the red blanket that covered her knees. The other was twisted into an arthritic claw.

Kate got up carefully and sat back in her seat, trying to keep her face neutral. "Doesn't look like you'll be hunting for a while," she murmured.

"I nearly died." Patience spat. She came to a halt

behind the metal desk. "Hate kept me going, girl. Kept me alive." Her face screwed up in contempt. "So keep talking, you little bitch, 'cause I'm hating you more all the time and it feels good."

Kate affected disinterest. "Come a long way to gloat, haven't you?"

"Not as far as your mama's come," Patience said.

Kate looked away, unable to hide her fear.

"She's caught an airplane; she's getting closer all the time." Patience cackled maliciously. "That's one little reunion I'd *hate* to miss. Besides, I was flown out here," the old woman added proudly. "Papa Takapa wanted to hear my tale in person."

That name again. "He wanted to hear about me and Tom?" Kate questioned.

"He arranged to have you picked up." Patience puffed herself up. "And he's chosen *me* to watch over you. He's got hideouts and strongholds all over the country—here, New York, Chicago. . . ."

"And are they all as crappy as this?" Kate shivered. "It's freezing in here."

Patience shook her head softly. "Got to keep the temperature steady. Papa Takapa's got *science* going on. . . ."

Kate was getting tired of this mystery man stuff. "Just who is this Takapa?"

"You'll be meeting him soon enough. He's the man who's going to turn things around for the 'wolf."

"Is that a fact?"

"Yes, it is." The old woman sounded deadly serious.

Kate puzzled for a moment over the name. *Takapa.* It felt like someone had just walked over her grave. "Takapa's a Navajo name, isn't it? What a poser. Bet his real name's Bob or something. He just throws around all this Native American crap so you'll all believe he's the Big Bad."

"Too much schooling in you, missy," Patience said disapprovingly. "You're plenty smart. But *man* smart, not 'wolf smart."

"I read a book tracing the history of silverbloods in 'wolf communities," Kate told her. The answer came to her. "Yes. The Atakapa were Navajo. They worshiped the wolf. And your Papa Takapa claims he's one of their descendants, I suppose?"

"He doesn't claim. He *is,*" Patience said sharply. "And they didn't *just* worship the wolf. You may know the tribe's name, but I wonder if you know its meaning."

Kate hid her fear under a noisy yawn.

Patience leaned forward and licked her lips. "It means 'Eaters of Men,' sugar."

## CHAPTER SIXTEEN

Tom sipped someone's abandoned coffee at the cybercafe. He'd hung around until someone left their terminal before their hour was up and slipped on himself. Time to see what Bloodlettings.com was about.

Almost disappointingly, it turned out to be a Louisiana real estate agency. The head guy's name was Adam Blood. Kind of a sick pun, Tom felt, but they had three branches, so it couldn't be harming business. He'd clearly underestimated how wacky the world of real estate was.

There was an address for the main office in New Orleans, in the Garden District. Tom finished the cold coffee with a grimace, then plucked an abandoned crust of sandwich from the next table and shoved that in his mouth too. It did little to stave off the hunger he felt, but perhaps nothing short of bringing down a herd of wildebeest could do that for him now.

*AB@Bloodlettings.com can help find Jicaque,* the note said.

"I hope so," Tom murmured. Then he left the café with a nod of thanks to the unimpressed staff.

He only hoped Adam Blood was working late tonight.

Tom's spirits, trampled to mush by his long, blistering walk through the cold streets, rose sharply when he saw the light blazing upstairs at the Bloodlettings branch shoehorned into a colorful parade of shops on Magazine Street.

He pressed the buzzer. When three short bursts brought no response, he kept his finger in place while counting slowly to sixty.

By the time he'd counted to twenty-two, an irritated male voice snapped out of the speaker grille by the door. "Yes? What?"

"I need to speak to Adam Blood," Tom said, and held his breath.

"You're speaking to him. We're closed."

Result. "May I come in? It's really urgent."

Blood sighed. "We open again at nine-thirty tomorrow morning."

His accent was weird—British? That would explain the "bloodlettings" pun. Tom took a deep breath. "It's about Jicaque."

The speaker grille remained silent. Then the door buzzed. Tom pushed it open. He trooped up the narrow stairs into a smart, well-lit office.

Adam Blood was as handsome as the teak desk he

sat behind. He was slim, probably mid-thirties, dressed in a stylish dark suit with a blue shirt and no tie. His brown hair was parted in the middle with floppy bangs, like he was trying to be Hugh Grant or something. He blinked his blue eyes in surprise as Tom came gingerly into the room, then jumped up in alarm.

"For God's sake," Blood fussed, "don't take another step until I've put down some paper. This carpet is Sumptuous Cream. It doesn't mix with Grimy Feet, all right?" He grabbed a selection of color brochures showing fancy houses in and around New Orleans and laid a trail over to a neat leather couch. "Now who the hell are you?"

"My name is Tom Anderson."

Blood gave him a long, thoughtful look. "Well, Tom Anderson, you're not here to buy or lease anything from me, are you?"

"No."

"Then I can drop the posh accent," said Blood cheerily in a rougher, broader voice. "Helps when you're shifting posh properties, but I bore myself arseless with it all day long."

Tom stared at him, bemused. "But you're still English, right?"

"Born and bred in London." He winked. "Just more Cockney than Kensington, if you catch my drift."

Tom didn't but decided not to dwell on it. "I, uh, think we have a mutual friend—Kate Folan?"

Blood stared at him blankly. "Kate who?"

Tom's hopes sank a little. "She thought you could help find Jicaque. She said, 'Troll Lover said so.'"

"Troll Lover!" Blood yelled, his face lighting up like a child's at Christmas. He clapped. "Good old Trolly! So you know her, do you?"

"Troll Lover is a girl?" Tom stared at him—and something clicked. Of course, Kate had told him she never used her real name when she was in those chat rooms. Could Troll Lover be one of her aliases? A stupid, made-up name that no one could trace back to her?

"I've been seeing a lot of her until recently," said Tom. "I think Kate Folan *is* Troll Lover. We came here together, but—"

"But this is brilliant!" Blood enthused. "Trolly's been a real help to me in my work!"

Now it was Tom's turn to frown. "She's helped you sell real estate?"

"No, my *work*. My real work. I do the property bit to pay the bills and because it's a good way of garnering, er, local knowledge." He gave a crooked smile. "I'm one of a group of what you might call mystic vigilantes. We keep tabs on the dark, satanic underbelly of the Crescent City. You know, the same as you do."

"Gotcha," said Tom, a little overwhelmed.

"Anyway, where is she, Kate the Troll Lover? And what's she like? Young? Old? Sexy?" Blood held up a hand, shut his eyes. "No, don't tell me. *She's* the troll, a big, fat bird with three chins; I just know she's—"

Tom cut across, raising his voice. "Skinny and dark haired, kind of cute, I guess—"

"Hallelujah!" Blood broke in.

"—and *way* too young for you. But she's in trouble. Big trouble. She's been kidnapped."

"You're kidding." Blood's face fell. "She's really too young for me?"

Tom wanted to grab Blood by the throat. *This* was the guy who could help them? "Look, did she ever tell you about the . . . uh, about the werewolves?"

Blood was suddenly grave. "Yeah, she did. She's an expert—pretty much everything I know about the lupine community comes from her." He looked at Tom expectantly. "So?"

"We kind of pissed off some 'wolves," Tom admitted. "They've been chasing after us. And now they've got Kate. They took her away somewhere."

"Dick of Diablo! The 'wolves are holding her? Are you sure?"

"Certain. I saw her my—"

"Wait. All that stuff on the news about a wild animal chasing a stolen ambulance through the warehouse district—you were mixed up in that?"

"Kind of," Tom half admitted.

"My cell phone's been ringing all day about that," Blood said. "So many people saw it, we figured it must be a hoax. But it fits. . . . My boys *told* me

something was going on with the 'wolves. . . ."
Abruptly Blood jumped up and began hopping about
as he pulled off first one shoe, then the other. A second bizarre ballet ensued as he inelegantly peeled off
his black socks and tossed them over to Tom.

"Right," he said. "Cover up those filthy bloody
feet so you can't tread dirt anywhere. We're going
uptown, to my place."

Tom eyed both Blood and the socks suspiciously.
"Why?"

"We need to find poor old Trolly now, as well as
your Jicaque, don't we?" said Blood, slipping his
bare feet back inside his leather loafers. "And the
ways and means are back at my place."

Tom waited nervously in the luxury of cotton
socks while Blood brought his car around from some
underground parking garage. Convincing Blood had
been easy. Too easy? What if he came back with
'wolves in tow? What if he was one himself?

Blood pulled up outside in a sleek silver BMW.
He was alone.

Tom opened the door and slid onto the soft
leather of the backseat. The luxury almost brought
tears to his eyes after his endless trekking around
the cluttered streets.

"So . . . why so keen to meet the old medicine
man?" Blood asked.

"I have a problem, and Kate thinks he's the only
one who can help me with it," Tom said guardedly.

"Secretive sod, aren't you," Blood said as he turned right onto a wide, tree-lined avenue. "Well, he's meant to be past it these days, old Jicaque. Of interest to die-hard enthusiasts only since the werewolves put him out of business."

"So he should be easier to find, right?" Tom said gruffly.

"True enough." Blood glanced at him and smiled. "My contacts have been digging about since Trolly mailed a few days back and they're quite hopeful. Jicaque's meant to be running a health food store or something." He grew pensive. "My contacts also informed me that something curious is happening in the lupine community. . . ."

"What?" asked Tom guardedly.

"Well, the community keeps pretty much to itself usually," Blood explained. "But someone's been trying to band them all together."

"Who?"

"I don't know. Funny name. Papa Smurf? Papa someone . . ."

Tom felt a shudder of apprehension. "Papa Takapa?"

Blood nodded, his frown deepening. "You've heard of him too?"

"Someone told me on a train," Tom muttered. "So how about you?" he asked, steering the subject away from himself. "You're from London, right? Why do you live here?"

"Came on holiday and didn't want to leave." Blood shrugged. "So I stayed."

"And you say you keep tabs on the weird stuff that goes down around here," Tom continued.

"You could say that."

"So what turned you on to it?"

"I lost friends to the weird stuff in this city," Blood replied, his voice neutral.

"Details?" Tom asked.

"You're just a kid," Blood said. "You don't want details."

"Uh-uh." Tom shook his head. "Too easy for you. If I'm going to trust you, I need to know why you're helping me now. What's in it for you?"

"A cynical little sod as well as secretive!"

*Comes from being dead for five weeks and losing half your humanity to a wolf,* Tom thought bitterly, but said nothing.

"Okay. Details. How about amateur voodoo cultists getting carried away with their sacrificial blades," Blood said mildly. "Or vampire wannabes who got their fondest wish granted." He paused. "Or a girlfriend who was turned werewolf."

Tom flinched. "What happened to her? Did she fight it, get turned back again?"

"She didn't want to turn back." Blood heaved a long sigh. "Werewolves bite to kill or else to turn a prospective mate. Seems she was bored with me and liked the lifestyle a hairier bloke could offer her."

"I'm sorry," Tom said.

"Me too. Killed off a bloody good relationship. As well as a number of the locals."

Tom was getting uneasy with Blood's offhand attitude. "So what, this stuff is all a joke to you?"

"No, it's not *all* a joke," said Blood mildly. "But if you don't laugh about it sometimes, you wind up screaming." He looked at Tom, blue eyes suddenly haunted. "Trust me on that."

*I want to trust you,* Tom thought.

"So, to fill my empty nights I looked into the whole supernatural deal a bit more. And scared myself witless." Blood shrugged. "Once I knew what was really going on round here, I couldn't just shut it all out again. I found I could only sleep at night if I was keeping an eye on things."

"You just watch?" Tom felt a lurch of disappointment. "You don't try to stop it?"

"I don't have a death wish," Blood said. "I'm no hero and neither are my friends in the group. All we try to do is help people who find themselves mixed up in stuff they don't really understand. Before it's too late for them. Or the poor sods who wind up their victims."

*It's too late for me,* Tom wanted to scream.

But Blood might not help him if he knew the truth.

Troubled, he gazed out of the window as they drove along leafy uptown streets, the darkness beaten back by ornate streetlights. He took in rows of towering wood-paneled and colonnaded mansions punctuated with narrow boxy dwellings and even humble cottages. The sight was both beautiful and sad at the same time.

Kate was never far from his thoughts.

At last Blood pulled up outside a discreetly elegant town house. "We're here."

Tom swung himself out of the car and followed Blood to the red front door. Six or seven locks glinted in the fuzzy glare of the streetlight across the road.

"Don't like this," muttered Blood. "Security lights aren't working. The place should be floodlit by now."

Tom tensed. Blood put a key to one of the locks. The door swung silently open.

"Someone's broken in," he murmured. He moved cautiously inside, flicked a switch.

Tom blinked in the sudden light. The hall and the living room beyond were decked out in pale and paler blues. There didn't seem to be an ornament in the place and there was barely any furniture. "Looks like you've been cleared out," he said.

"It's tastefully minimalist, you cheeky young swine," huffed Blood, slipping back into his posh voice for a second. "And this wasn't an ordinary break-in. My home office is upstairs; that's where they'll have made for."

"They?" Tom echoed.

"Those 'wolves you pissed off, remember them?"

Blood stomped up the stairs to the landing. "I think they're taking it out on me. . . ." He threw open a heavy wooden door and stopped dead. "That was an understatement."

Tom stared in dismay around the open, airy office. It had been totally trashed. Chairs and tables lay smashed or toppled. The floor was strewn with files and papers and photographs, with books and shattered bric-a-brac. A computer monitor, its connecting wires ripped out, had fallen facedown in the sea of debris as if unable to stare out over the carnage any longer.

Then Tom noticed that Blood was staring at something else across the room. He looked in the same direction. A message had been daubed in crimson over one tastefully pale cream wall.

JICAQUE STAYS OUT OF IT IF YOU WANT GIRL TO LIVE
AWAIT FURTHER INSTRUCTIONS
WE'RE WATCHING YOU

## CHAPTER SEVENTEEN

"Gorgon knockers," breathed Blood. He stared about, taking in the damage, his brown hair flopping about frantically like it was having its own private drama. "Seems my subtle inquiries about the old medicine man haven't been as subtle as I thought." He glanced at Tom. "Or else they saw you come to me and popped round to prepare a welcome."

"I'm sorry," said Tom, ashen faced. "This is my fault."

"Yeah, it is," Blood said sharply. Then he sighed. "Look, don't give yourself a hernia. New Orleans is probably the only city on earth where insurance firms will actually cover you for 'acts of the supernatural.'"

"They could kill Kate." Tom paced restlessly. "What are we going to do?"

Blood looked at him warily. "Before we rush off into any other serious messes, I think you should tell me exactly what's going on. Like how you got involved with these bloody 'wolves—miserable, murdering, flea-ridden—"

"I'm one of them," Tom blurted.

Blood took an instinctive jump back, skidding on an old paperback and almost falling over as he did so. "You're lupine?" He glanced out at the night sky through the window nervously, then snapped his fingers. "*You're* the one who ran through the city. . . ."

"That's right. The 'wolves after us are Kate's parents and their network. Purebloods. They turned me as a mate for her. She's pureblood too, but her 'wolf's not activated yet. It's why I need to see Jicaque. I need the cure."

Blood nodded and sat down nervously on the upturned monitor. "Well, while we wait for 'further instructions,' you'd better tell me everything." He sighed heavily. "I suspect this is going to be a very long night."

The dim light stayed sullenly on in Kate's storeroom cell, the drowsy hum of the cooling systems never faltering. She wondered how long she'd been here, chained to the seat. Every time her eyes slipped shut, Patience would snap at her to wake up, jolting her back into reality. Or else she'd produce the key to Kate's chain with a cruel smile, place it on the table almost within reach, then hide it from sight in her blouse pocket.

Now the old woman watched her from across the desk, sipping from a steaming cup of coffee. "Mmm, I can't get enough of that caffeine kick," she murmured, setting the cup down with her twisted hand and pouring more from a thermos. "I can do without blood for a time if I have to, but fresh ground? No way." She chuckled. "Bet you're thirsty, right?"

Kate nodded.

Patience leaned forward over the desk and spat in her face. "Drink it all down, now," she said softly.

Kate wiped her cheek with her sleeve, fighting back the panic that threatened to overwhelm her. She was trapped here, surrounded by 'wolves, while her mother drew ever closer, like a gathering darkness.

There had to be something she could do.

"Laugh while you can, Patience," she said as she slipped her hands in her pockets and discreetly searched their contents. Lip gloss. A wallet. "You've told Bob—sorry, Takapa—all you know, and now you've been assigned guard duty to a girl who's already chained up. It's about all an old cripple like you can manage, right?"

*Brass knuckles?* Right, from the guy in the Jack O'Lantern mask.

"Shut up," Patience growled.

Kate slid the linked metal rings onto her fingers and continued her exploration of the other pocket. "So when they're through with me here," she said, "you can bet they'll be through with you too." Two quarters. Skull ring. "You failed, Patience. You let us go, you drew attention to your kind. You're of more value to Takapa as meat than as anything else."

"I said shut up!" Patience yelled. But Kate could see the dull spark of fear in her eyes.

A loud buzzer sounded suddenly, silencing them both. The door. They stared at it in horror.

Kate's fingers squeezed instinctively around the skull ring in her hand. With a click it popped open against her fingers.

Patience maneuvered her chair around and wheeled herself slowly over to the door.

Seizing her chance, Kate pulled out the ring. The skull part was hollow and hinged. It clipped down over a tiny, hidden container. There were two crumbling white tablets nestled inside. She tipped them out into her hand for a closer look. They could be aspirin. Or they could be something a lot more potent—for dropping in the drink of some poor unsuspecting girl at a bar?

Kate looked up at Patience, a new fierceness inside her as a desperate plan began to form.

"Who's there?" Patience demanded of the door.

"Takapa."

The voice was cold and emotionless. It stabbed at Kate's insides. She concealed the tablets under her thigh, closed up the ring, and quickly slipped it on her finger as Patience entered a four-digit code on a keypad. The door opened a fraction. The old woman skittered back in her chair.

Nothing happened for a moment.

Then a massive werewolf, lean, sinewy, and pure

white, burst into the room with a terrifying roar.

The huge white beast went for Kate so quickly she had no time to scream. It reared up over her, eyes narrowed in malice, rancid drool pouring from the ponderous jaws. She shut her eyes, put her hands over her face in a futile gesture to keep it away.

There was a rushing, eerie cracking sound, like ghosts bundling up a pile of dry sticks.

"Boo."

Kate opened her eyes.

She decided maybe she preferred the 'wolf.

A naked man stood before her, early fifties, maybe, stick thin and covered in eczema. He looked half starved: his ribs stuck out like blades through flaky skin, his stomach was sunken, his hips protruded like bone handles.

Kate swiftly looked up at the man's face. It was a corpse-like white, his features bunched up together in the middle of his face. His white-blond hair was shaved back to stubble. A silver double helix dangled from the fleshy lobe of his right ear, while his left ear looked like it had been chewed clean off. His skin was pockmarked with the scars of old acne, and his eyes were a watery pink, the color of raw flesh.

An albino lupine. Rare. Ugly.

And from the way Patience was trembling in her chair, very, very dangerous.

"Make you jump, did I?" said Takapa, smiling. His nasal voice carried a trace of accent. German, perhaps. "You know, I could've gone further in my change. I can push my body all the way to wolf so not a trace of my man self remains."

"It's got to be an improvement," Kate muttered scathingly.

"Show some respect," Patience snapped at her. "It's beautiful."

Takapa ignored her, focusing fully on Kate. "Still. Why bother to impress you when I can simply make you fear me?" He bared his yellow teeth, sharpened to fine points. "Welcome, Marcie's little girl."

"I'm Kate Folan," Kate said, meeting his gaze. "And on the subject of names, you don't seem much like a papa to me. You don't seem to take much care of yourself, so how are your deluded 'children' supposed to cope?"

"You've got spirit," said Takapa mildly. "I like that."

"That makes my day," Kate muttered. "So you'd just love it if I said, 'Let me out of here, you freakish son of a bitch'?"

Takapa giggled. Much to Kate's relief, he scooped up the robe he must have discarded just outside the door and slipped it on. It clung to his skeletal form like wet silk on a scarecrow. "Let you out? But you've only just arrived. I'm so glad you've come to me. You and your lovely wereling."

Kate shifted uneasily in her chair. "Tom, you mean? He's nothing. Just some silverblood Mom fished out of the river."

Takapa walked up to the chair and crouched down in front of her. She squirmed as he leaned in close to her. "Good. You'll soon forget him, then."

Abruptly he got up, walked over to one of the crates on the nearby rack, and pried off the lid. He scooped out a mass of crimson slush ice and pushed it greedily into his mouth like it was Ben & Jerry's or something. "Mmm." He shut his eyes and sighed dreamily. "Love it when you get a clot."

He held some under Kate's nose. "Slush pop? It's blood, liver, and chili sauce, my own recipe."

"You sick bastard." Kate turned away. She saw Patience looking hungrily at the gruesome snack.

Takapa threw some at the old woman like a snowball. It hit her on the chest, and he snickered as she desperately lapped it up from her baggy blouse.

Kate's stomach heaved. She closed her eyes. She wanted to hide away inside herself and never come out again. But Takapa grabbed hold of her hair with slushy fingers and yanked her head back. She gasped, flinched as he leaned in on her, as she smelled his rank breath.

"I'm being kind to you, sweetheart," he said. "Retribution's coming for you. You should be grateful that Papa Takapa wants to treat you kindly." He relaxed his grip on her hair and ran his fingers through it. "But then, I suppose you've brought me a gift, haven't you? Your reluctant 'wolf friend." A dreamy smile fleshed itself out on Takapa's scarred face. "A wereling prefigures the coming of Wolf Time. He shall devour his dominant humanity, give himself over to the wolf forever. A first sacrifice that will turn all the world over to our kind."

Kate glowered up at him. "Even assuming your stupid myths *were* true, Tom isn't that person."

"So, you don't believe the old stories?" Takapa steepled his fingers and began to circle her with slow, deliberate steps. "Humans just aren't superstitious anymore, have you noticed? Their world is so scientific." He laughed. "But science works for 'wolves too. We can use their technologies against them." He gestured at the crates and boxes lining his chilled storeroom. "A process I've already begun."

Kate glanced nervously around the walls. The generator hum seemed to grow creepily louder, a dark energy straining to be free. "I take it this place is more than just a fridge full of snacks. What's in those boxes?"

"Experiments . . . research . . . our future." Takapa tapped the side of his nose. "Did you know they used to tell a man's future from the entrails of a chicken?" he said wistfully, as if recalling the good old days. "But his *own* entrails will do—if you study them on a genetic level. I'm sure we can foretell the future for your brave wereling."

Kate vowed she wouldn't give this monster the satisfaction of knowing how petrified she felt. "You know, science also gave us concealer sticks and colored contact lenses. If you used *those* human technologies, you might not look like such a freak."

"I don't hide what I am," Takapa said simply, and something in his cold tone made her glad he hadn't risen to her bait. "Not like you. She-wolf." He sniffed the air in front of her thoughtfully. "No, you're not quite ripened yet, are you, Kate? But soon the wolf inside you will be drawn out."

Kate cringed as he licked her face.

Takapa's cherry eyes were bright and hungry. "I'll be waiting. With your wereling out of the picture, your mama will need to find you another mate."

"No." Kate couldn't keep the quiver from her voice.

"Oh yes." Takapa nodded, then paced over to the door. "Your mother could prove very useful to me. And a blood tie . . ." He chuckled, rubbed his hands. "That would ensure me a presence among the Old Name elite."

"You think my mother would let a nameless freak like you piss in the family gene pool?" Kate spat at him. "And you think I wouldn't kill myself before I let some ugly, anorexic white thing like you touch me?"

Fangs poked through Takapa's thin-lipped smile. "You're going to be a beautiful bride." He turned to go.

"What should I do, Papa?" Patience asked submissively. She made a pathetic figure, blouse stained and wet, hunched up in the chair with all her stitches and bruises.

"I already told you what to do," Takapa said quietly, though he kept his eyes on Kate. "Watch her. See that she behaves. Don't let her hurt herself before her mother has the chance."

Patience nodded. "But what about after? I mean, I got no home I can go to and . . ." She trailed off as Takapa simply turned and left. The door clicked shut behind him.

"Looks like you don't figure highly in his plans." Kate gave Patience a scornful smile. "Wonder what'll happen to you when my mother comes."

Patience glared at her and took a swig from the coffee. "You'd do better to worry about yourself, missy."

"Me?" Kate gave her a big, wide-eyed smile, sat on her hands, and began quietly grinding the tablets she'd hidden there against the edge of the chair. She felt them crumbling to a lumpy powder under her fingers.

*Just how paranoid are you, Patience?* she wondered, knowing now she had just one chance to get out of here alive.

## Chapter Eighteen

Tom was woken by the sound of fingers tapping out an erratic rhythm over a keyboard. Rubbing his eyes, he saw Adam Blood dressed in a black silk kimono. He was sitting on a slashed footstool, a laptop perched awkwardly on his knees. A modem cord snaked through the chaos covering the floor to where a phone jack must be hidden.

"Good, you're awake," Blood snapped without looking up.

"Why?" Tom asked, rubbing his neck, stiff from a night on the unyielding leather couch.

"Because I need coffee. Kitchen. Downstairs. Now."

Tom stretched noisily. "What are you doing?"

"The note says we can't find Jicaque." Blood looked up, the ghost of a smile playing over his lips. "It doesn't say the same about Kate, does it? And Marcie Folan's not the only one who can put out the word."

"You've got your friends on the case!" Tom sat up, excited.

"Better yet," Blood told him, "your story of last

night persuaded me to swallow my pride, find the number in my little black book, and contact my late, lamented ex, Lydia."

Tom's heart sank. "The woman who was turned?"

Blood nodded. "That's the one."

"But she's one of *them!*" Tom shouted, appalled. "What if she knows Takapa and tells him you've been snooping—?"

"Hello? Earth to Tom!" Blood gave him a dark look. "I didn't have to do any snooping, all right? I just called her late last night and made out I was worried the wolf rampaging through the central business district yesterday was her. That it had made me realize I still cared about her, remembered the good times, and blah de blah de blah. You know, women love that crap."

Tom folded his arms. "And?"

"And Lydia was knocked out! She's single, as it happens! Split from the 'wolf boyfriend ages back!" He punched the air. "I knew it wouldn't last!"

Tom stared at Blood in disbelief. "Why so happy? You'd actually date someone you knew was lupine?"

"Not necessarily *date* them. But I told you, Tom, I'm no hero. I do what's practical." He gestured around his ruined office. "And after this little warning, I want a friend in the lupine camp. Someone who can help me out if things get tricky." He pointed at the gory message on the wall. "If they *are* watching me and they see me with someone on their side, so much the better."

Tom could see how Blood was turning the situation to his advantage. "So how does Kate figure in all this?" he demanded, beginning to lose patience.

"Lydia told me that yesterday's events caused a real ruckus in the local lupine community. Apparently this bloke Takapa is going to address a gathering of 'wolves at noon today, at a conference center downtown."

"Why?" Tom wondered. "What for?"

"Who cares?" Blood shrugged. "You're missing the point. Something big's happening—and Takapa will be there. And so will I. I've offered to give Lydia a lift to the gathering. If Takapa *has* taken Kate prisoner, and let's face it, it's likely . . ."

Tom felt a shiver run down his spine. "You think she could be there too?"

"There's a chance. And if not, some of my friends can follow Takapa back to the stone he crawled out from under and see who else is there. I'm just e-mailing them now." Blood grinned, showing impeccable white teeth. "Hooray for me."

"I thought you weren't a hero?" Tom raised an eyebrow. "Eavesdropping on a secret gathering of all the lupines in Louisiana might be just a bit dangerous, don't you think?"

"That's right, you look on the bright side," grumbled Blood. "I'm still reeling from the sheer genius of my plan, okay? I'll worry about the implications later."

A tinny chime sounded from his laptop.

"You've got mail," said Tom.

Blood double-clicked on the e-mail and then stared at his screen like it had just slapped him in the face. "Hell's buttocks, they've actually done it." He frowned. "But I thought Blake was away?"

"What are you talking about?"

"Jicaque." Blood's brilliant blue eyes drilled into Tom's. "My lads have probably put their lives on the line, but they've found Jicaque!"

Tom looked at him, slack jawed. "You're kidding me."

He shook his head. "My pal Blake has come up with an address on Chartres Street. Makes sense for a medicine man; it's close to the historic Pharmacy Museum—"

"Never mind the realtor spiel," Tom said, his heart racing with the prospect of a cure. A warning voice told him not to get his hopes up, but they were already straining for the sky. "What do we do? What the hell do we do? They're watching us; we can't just stroll out and visit him, can we? And what about Kate, I mean—"

"The first thing *you* do is calm down." Blood checked his watch. "There are four hours till noon, and it's better I'm not seen with you when I go to pick up Lydia."

"But if you're going to find Kate, I should be there!" Tom protested.

Blood shook his head. "We have to tread carefully," he said, "or we could put her in more danger. So, why don't you slip out and make contact with Jicaque?"

He tugged some printer paper from beneath a stack of phone directories and found a fountain pen. "Probably safest to take the St. Charles streetcar from the stop round the corner," he said, scrawling out a map in peacock blue ink. "It's not quick, but it's very public. Get off at Canal Street, and run the rest of the way." He handed Tom ten dollars and started searching again among the debris on the floor. "Now, you'll need some shoes, of course. What size are you?"

"Ten," said Tom, gazing at the scribbled map like it was a hundred-dollar bill.

"I'm a ten too, but a U.K. ten. That's an American eleven." He frowned as he hauled out some white Converses from beneath a broken bookshelf. "So these will be too big, but then, I'm not a gentleman's outfitter." He chucked the shoes at Tom. "Well, what are you waiting for? Get out of here!"

Tom slipped on one of the sneakers but recoiled from the other. "What's that smell?" He turned the sneaker over and something fell out. It looked like a mummified chili, stuffed with pungent herbs and spices and tied with a ribbon.

"Oh, just gris-gris," Blood explained. Was it

Tom's imagination, or did Blood suddenly look a little shifty? "A voodoo charm someone gave me."

"Voodoo?" Tom wrinkled his nose. "Smells more like dog doo."

"Take it with you," Blood suggested. "Christ knows we'll need all the luck we can get. The 'wolves want Jicaque to stay hidden, remember? They could be watching."

Tom wriggled his foot into the other sneaker. "I'll be careful."

"And don't forget, Tom, even if you *can* persuade Jicaque to help . . ." Blood sighed. "This cure, whatever it is . . . chances are it won't be quick *or* pleasant. So make contact, suss out the lay of the land, and get yourself back here. I'll call to let you know what's happening. Now come on, let's go and make a scene outside for anyone watching."

"Okay." Tom nodded, hesitated in the doorway. "Uh . . ."

"Thanks?" Blood shook his head. "Thank me when all this is over and done with. Okay?"

Kate wished she had some way of telling time. She felt like she'd been cooped up here all night, and she didn't dare wait much longer. She had to act.

Patience had been brought a plate of food and allowed a bathroom break, but no guard had come to relieve her.

"You know the code to open the door," Kate had

taunted her. "Why don't you just roll away? I'm sick of the sight of you."

"Keep your mouth shut," was Patience's gloomy response. Maybe she was starting to realize she was as much of a prisoner in Takapa's lair as Kate was. More brooding than angry now, Patience had drifted for hours between sullen, sleepy silence and bouts of rattling snores. The sound punctuated Kate's own fitful sleep like machine-gun fire.

At last the old woman opened her eyes. She snorted as she took in her surroundings and glared at Kate. Automatically she unscrewed the thermos and poured herself another cup of thick, syrupy coffee.

Kate kept her face quietly neutral. Then she looked at the door and allowed her expression to change to one of fleeting surprise.

Patience noticed and turned swiftly to look for herself.

Kate darted out her hand, held it hovering over the plastic cup on the desk.

Patience turned and saw her.

Kate let her eyes widen with alarm, started to snatch back her hand.

But Patience lunged and grabbed hold of her powdery fingers. "What's this?" she growled.

"Nothing." Kate yanked her hand clear.

Patience swore and wheeled herself around the desk. "You tried to put something in my coffee!"

"What do you mean, *tried?*" Kate smirked, with a conspicuous glance down at the skull ring. "Every time you fell asleep, I dropped in some more. And every time you woke up, you chugged it right down."

Patience narrowed her eyes.

Kate displayed the skull ring a little more prominently, hoping the old woman would catch on.

Finally she did. "Let me see that."

"No," Kate protested like she meant it, but the old woman wrenched the ring from her finger.

Patience soon figured out the hinged skull lid, even with her injured hand. She dipped her finger in the chalky remains of pill hidden inside. "What have you done to me?" she hissed.

"You want to know?" Kate rattled her leg. "Undo this chain."

"No way, missy."

"Then I guess you'll just have to find out the hard way."

Patience narrowed her eyes even further. "Tell me."

"All right." Kate shrugged, prepared herself for an epic lie. "It's poison powder. Suicide to go, from a backroom pharmacist in Salt Lake. They were meant for Tom and me if we got caught, if there was no other way out." She smiled sweetly. "But you've been such a pal, I thought I'd save it for you."

Patience brushed the white powder from her thick fingers like it was burning her.

"It shouldn't take long now," Kate went on. She leaned forward and lowered her voice to a confidential murmur. "Can you feel the poison inside you? Soaking into your blood, building up in your veins—"

Patience raised her fist.

"Takapa told you I wasn't to be harmed," Kate cried hastily. "Touch me one more time and I'll never tell you the antidote."

The old woman hesitated. "Antidote?"

"Sure. It's easy to counteract the chemicals if you know what they are." Kate gave a bitter laugh. "I'm plenty smart, remember? Too much schooling—you said so yourself."

"Papa Takapa will make you tell me."

Kate shook her head. "I doubt it. And even if you were worth his trouble, you'll be dead inside an hour unless you listen to me."

Patience seemed paralyzed with fear and indecision. Kate could almost hear the paranoid thoughts running through her mind as all the little fears about her own worth kicked violently into play.

Finally she slumped back in her wheelchair and stared at Kate. Her eyes welled up, her nose started to run, and she massaged her gut like she was getting cramps. "Tell me the cure. I don't want to die. Tell me."

*Gotcha.* Kate felt no sense of triumph at tricking this scared, pitiful creature, and she was a long way from being safely out of here. But as she held her hand out for the key to her chain, a few embers of hope deep inside her flared into fire.

Patience quickly handed her the key. "But remember," she said, "only I know the code to this door. If you don't tell me how to fix myself up, it stays shut."

Kate massaged the bruised flesh of her ankle, numbed by the metal shackles. "Don't think so. We need to reach a drugstore, and fast. Get me out of here."

"They'll never let you leave!" squealed Patience.

Kate just shrugged. "Time's running out for both of us, Patience. But I promise you'll go before me."

Patience angrily punched in the code on the pad. "Walk ahead of me. Come on, hurry."

Kate's heart was pounding so hard she thought any guards would be able to hear her coming. But the clean, clinical, windowless corridors they moved down were all empty. "Where is everyone?" she whispered cautiously.

"They can't have cleared out," Patience muttered. "There was some kind of big gathering going to happen, but they'd have taken me—"

"You must get it by now," said Kate quietly. "You don't matter to them anymore. And now that you've set me free, there's no going back for you either."

They went on. The whole place remained silent and empty until a turn in the passage revealed a set of fire doors, laxly guarded by two men slumped in chairs. One was a good-looking Asian. The other was ugly and white with long blond hair and a face scored with vivid gashes. With a shock Kate recognized him as the fake porter who'd helped kidnap her back on the train and who'd been taken away in the ambulance once they'd reached New Orleans.

"Takapa must be low on staff if he has to keep wheeling out his 'wolf wounded for guard duty," Kate observed quietly.

"They're not 'wolves," Patience sneered. "Just wannabes. But first they have to prove themselves to Takapa, do whatever he tells them."

Kate nodded. It figured that they were the only ones left there if a big 'wolf gathering was going on. She leaned over to Patience and hissed in her ear, "Just get us past them."

Before Kate realized what she was doing, Patience slammed her palm into the fire alarm on the wall. A deafening shriek wailed out from a siren somewhere in the ceiling.

Kate clapped her hands over her ears, her heart pounding. What if the place wasn't really empty? She peeked around the corner, watching tensely as Patience heaved herself forward in her wheelchair and rolled up to the guards. The men had jumped up and were staring about uncertainly.

"The storeroom!" Patience yelled. "The girl started a fire there!" She slapped the Asian guy's backside. "Quick, before all Papa's work gets roasted!"

The man started running toward Kate's hiding place. He would see her in seconds. No time to think. As he turned the corner, Kate swung her fist into his face. She shouted out in pain, but the guard went down soundlessly.

Kate looked down at the brass knuckles loose on her slender hand, then at the prone body at her feet. "I think it hurt me almost as much as it hurt you," she muttered.

Patience was waiting by the doors, the blond guy sprawled on the floor beside her, clutching his face. Her good hand was wet with his blood.

"I think those cuts of his might still be tender," Patience said. She sucked her bloody fingers like Popsicles as Kate unbolted the doors.

Seconds later they were outside in an alleyway, blinking in the September sunlight. Kate slammed the fire doors shut and wedged a length of wood through the large metal handles, trapping both the men and the noisy alarms inside. Then she felt Patience grab hold of her jacket.

"So?" The old woman looked up at her.

"So, nothing," Kate said coldly. "There's nothing wrong with you, Patience."

"You're lying," Patience croaked, tears spilling down her lined face.

"I never drugged you," Kate told her. "Sure, there

were pills inside the ring. But I never put them into your coffee. It was all just a bluff."

A flare of yellow spun through Patience's eyes, but somehow Kate knew that Patience wouldn't attack her. It wasn't just that the old woman was weakened and wheelchair-bound. There was despair written in the set of her shoulders. Kate knew from bitter experience the anguish of being betrayed and used by your own family.

For several seconds Patience seemed frozen as a statue, staring into space. Then she nodded slowly and let go of Kate's jacket.

"The old ways are changing," she said, and she might've been any ordinary old lady lamenting the lost years. "The community . . . the ties that bind us . . . it's all breaking down."

"And Papa Takapa wants to build a new community in its place," mused Kate.

Patience sighed. "Well, I guess we're both on the run now."

"Good luck," Kate said without much conviction.

"I figure they won't be so bothered about finding an old wreck like me," Patience concluded. Her tone became sly. "But you'd better watch your back, little girl. 'Cause your momma's claws are going to be reaching out for you everywhere you go."

Kate turned to leave.

"I'm a survivor!" Patience yelled after her, rocking

in her wheelchair. "I'll be fine! But how about you, huh? *How about you?*"

Kate didn't look back. She forced herself to stay calm and walked briskly down to the quiet street at the end of the lane.

Where was Tom right now? Where was her mother?

Her brisk walk became a jog, and the jog became a desperate, panicked run into the heedless heart of the city.

## CHAPTER NINETEEN

Adam Blood physically threw Tom out onto the street. "I'm not getting mixed up in this!" he yelled. "You got yourself into it, get yourself out of it!" He gave Tom a covert wink, then shooed him away. "Now move it!"

Tom ran away down the leafy avenue in his oversized shoes. He'd memorized the map, and soon he could hear the clang and rumble of an approaching streetcar. He looked around carefully as he boarded and sat down on the hard mahogany seat. No one was paying him any attention.

The streetcar pulled slowly away. A cool breeze blew in through the large windows. Tom could barely sit still. He'd know soon if he had a chance to put this nightmare behind him. Quite literally, to start living again. He pictured himself bursting through the back door of his home and the looks on his parents' faces as they realized he was alive and well. Grabbing his brother in one of the old wrestling hugs they used to give each other.

But what about Kate? Even if Blood could rescue Kate from her captors, Marcie would still want revenge on her and Tom. And if Tom lost his lupine strength, would he be able to protect them both?

Tom shook his head. *You have to do this,* he told himself. *Whatever it costs, you have to.*

Outside, people were heading off to work, shop-keepers were sweeping the pavement outside their stores, kids with heavy backpacks were walking to school. The view seemed oddly out of place with the old-fashioned wood-and-brass styling of the streetcar. It trundled on agonizingly slowly. *Be patient,* Tom told himself.

He was still telling himself over and over as he finally pushed his way off the crowded streetcar at Canal Street and ran toward his destination.

Once he'd found the pharmacy museum, Tom looked quickly around, panting for breath. He soon located the address Blood had given him: a health food store nestled in a colorful façade a few doors down.

Tom paused. What if this was another trap? Could Blood have set him up?

"Where y'at?"

The voice made Tom jump. He remembered the creepy old man hiding out at the back of the dilapi-dated movie theater. But the accent was different, more foreign, the voice younger.

"You look like someone who waits with purpose."

The speaker was a man pushing fifty, with graying hair pulled back in a ponytail. He wore a brightly colored coat with simple, faded garments beneath. He looked like a younger, somehow more authentic version of the man in the movie theater.

"Jicaque?" Tom murmured.

The man reacted, gave Tom a look he couldn't fathom.

"My name is Tulung," he said at last. "Will you come?"

Tom cautiously followed the man down a narrow alley to the back of the building and up a fire escape to the second floor.

"Whispered questions have been asked all around the city," Tulung told him. "Jicaque knows that someone is looking for him."

"Will he see me?" Tom asked quickly. "It's important."

"It is dangerous. For you both." Tulung stopped and looked over his shoulder at Tom. "But I feel courage in you. And I know Jicaque's courage."

He led Tom into a small kitchen that smelled strongly of spices. Beyond was a large, chilly room that had to be Jicaque's work space. Weird abstract paintings lined the terra-cotta walls, hanging over benches piled high with mystical-looking clutter, bubbling beakers, everything a practicing medicine man might need, save for a full-on cauldron. A blue door bisected the wall to Tom's left, charms and chains and ribbons hanging from a hundred hooks in the old wood. In the center of the room was a large, square red mat decorated with swirling golden symbols. At each corner rose a towering abstract sculpture, twisted and strange. The morning sunlight caught on their heavy bronze bodies through two tall open windows, around which gauzy curtains fluttered.

Incongruous on one of the benches was a gleaming new computer with printer, scanner, and webcam.

Tulung could see Tom was intrigued. "Technology is a tool, like any other," he said.

"I guess we all have to move with the times," Tom said politely, but he could barely hide his impatience. "Where is Jicaque?"

"I am here."

The voice was weak and weary with age. Tom spun around to find that the blue door had opened soundlessly. A wizened old man stood glowering in the doorway, his puny frame swamped by heavy, elaborately embroidered robes in blue and gold. His eyes were rheumy and gray as the wisps of hair that hung down to his hunched shoulders. He looked down the end of his hooked nose at Tom and seemed to be in a bad temper.

"You're risking both our lives by searching me out," the old man rasped. "You shouldn't have bothered."

Tom stared. "You're Jicaque?"

The old man nodded, then lifted his hands. "I won't help you."

"Please, at least hear me out." Tom realized he was almost shouting. Disappointment clawed at his hopes. He'd imagined Jicaque in his mind to be some great, powerful magical figure, a storybook magician, striking and inspiring—not some shriveled-up old man who could barely keep upright under the weight of his robe.

"Very well," said the old man at last. He hobbled over to his red mat and sank stiffly into a cross-legged position.

Tulung ushered Tom forward to sit before Jicaque.

"I've been turned 'wolf," said Tom briefly, bitterly. "Against my will. I fought against it. My friend, she says I'm a silverblood, or a wereling, or—"

Jicaque waved him silent. His eyes were shut tight. "I feel the force inside you. Powerful—it almost breaks the air." He cocked his head. "I can hear it howling. Gathering strength. But I can't interfere. I don't dare."

"The 'wolf's getting stronger?" Tom stared at him in horror. "Please, you *must* help me!"

"Even I can feel it," said Tulung, anxiously studying his master's face. "If that kind of power falls into Takapa's hands . . ."

Jicaque's eyes snapped open. He gazed unfathomably at Tom for a full thirty seconds. Then he said, "You're right, Tulung. Yes, you're right. We must act at once to exorcise this spirit."

"An exorcism?" Tom rubbed his forehead, confused. So was Jicaque going to help him, then? What, exactly, had made him change his mind? "You can really just . . . talk it out of me?"

"We must bind him, Tulung," announced Jicaque, rising with some effort.

"Bind me?" Tom echoed. "Now, wait just a—"

"It is one of the seven Rituals of the Troubled Wolf," said Tulung softly. "Your spirit is entwined with the wolf spirit. The two must be untangled with charms and incantations. We give each a voice. Then each can argue for the governing of your body and soul."

"What if I lose?" Tom whispered.

"We will chant with you. With Jicaque chanting on your behalf, your voice will be louder, stronger. The wolf will flee."

Tom turned back to Jicaque. Draped over the old man's arms was a wolf pelt, larger by far than the one that had been stretched over his mattress at the Folans' house. It smelled musky and old.

"No," Tom said. Bile rose in his throat. "You can't make me wear that. Please."

"It will give the wolf voice without changing your form," said Jicaque.

"I need time to think this through." Tom backed away. "My friend—"

"You don't dare delay!" Jicaque bellowed. Tom could hardly believe that such a voice could come from so small a frame.

Faster than Tom would have believed possible, the old man's hand streaked up. Tom gasped as something scratched against his shoulder. He stared. Jicaque was holding a thorn with a moist, glistening tip.

"It will help you relax, ready you for the struggle ahead," said Jicaque. "There's so little time."

Tom's vision began to blur as the old man advanced with the wolf pelt.

Kate was being herded somewhere.

She knew it wasn't just coincidence that the same men in dark business suits kept appearing in her path, forcing her to take another turn. And there was a woman behind her, nondescript in black jeans and a sweater, who stopped when she stopped, who matched her pace when she walked on.

Now Kate wished she'd kept running at random through this warren of vast, moldering brick warehouses instead of stopping to try and get her bearings. She'd given them time to track her. And now they were forcing her to some unknown destination. Every time she tried to take an unexpected path, a figure would stand at the end of the path and shake its head.

Her plan was to contact Adam Blood somehow

to see if Tom had been in touch. She clung to the forlorn hope that the note she'd stuffed in Tom's jeans pocket was still there and that Tom had actually seen it. But Kate knew that if the 'wolves were back on to her, she didn't stand a chance. And there weren't enough people around these crumbling fringes of the old warehouse district to offer any sort of protection. No crowds in which to lose herself.

No witnesses.

She wondered if these were 'wolves or wannabes on her tail. The brass knuckles still hung loosely around her fingers, but the thought of using it again made her feel sick. Besides, she doubted her pursuers would patiently form a line for her to punch them all out.

Suddenly, as if at some secret signal, the woman trailing Kate broke into a run, coming for her.

Kate ran too, veering off down a side street. Two drunks slumped against a wall watched her pelting approach without surprise or concern.

Then one of them stuck out his leg and tripped her.

Kate fell sprawling onto the hard pavement. Her palms stung with the impact. She heard the two drunks laughing and the sound of the woman's footsteps getting louder. Kate hurried up and off again, convinced that any second now a man in a dark business suit would appear as if by magic to block her way at the end of the street.

But it was actually two men who strode calmly into view.

Kate spun around. The woman, seeing that the way ahead was blocked, had slowed her pace to a fast walk. She was flanked on either side by the drunks, who now walked with a menacing sense of purpose. All three were smiling.

Kate turned back to the men barring her way. "I've got money," she said desperately. "Please, don't let them hurt me!"

The men looked at each other, amused. In that second of distraction Kate delivered a kick in the groin to the man nearest her. As he doubled up in pain, she leapfrogged over him and into the busier street beyond. But the other man had grabbed hold of her arm and was pulling her back into the side street.

"Fire!" Kate yelled to some people walking on the other side of the street. "Help me, there's a fire!" She knew people would be more up for tackling a blaze than five aggressors in a dark alley. But still no one took notice. They probably thought she was nuts or fooling around and being restrained by her nice, respectable-looking father.

Kate saw her captor's eyes flash yellow through the shades he wore as he tightened his grip on her wrist.

Then suddenly she heard a car braking hard. It whistled to a stop alongside her, and a handsome man with clear blue eyes and wildly waving hair leapt out.

"Do you need assistance?" he asked in a precise, British accent. But Kate realized with a shock he was asking the man who held her prisoner.

"Everything's cool," the man assured him.

"Please, I insist. Let me give you a hand," the smooth guy said. Then he hit Kate's captor full in the face. "Ow!" he bellowed as the man went down. "You could've taken your sunglasses off!" He turned to Kate, rubbing his fist, and gave her a rueful smile. "Troll Lover, I presume?"

Kate grinned so wide her lips cracked. "Adam Blood?"

"The same." He gestured to his car. "You'd better jump in."

The woman in black jeans peered out from the side street, presumably wondering what was taking her accomplice so long to haul Kate back out of sight. In seconds she and the two fake drunks were running for Blood's car.

Kate threw herself in the back. Blood pulled away with a screech of tires before she could even close her door properly. It flew back open into one of the drunks and sent him reeling into the woman. Then Blood swung the car around the corner and her pursuers were lost from view.

"Adam, for God's sake!" came an aggrieved voice from the front of the car.

For the first time Kate noticed the elegant, well-dressed blonde in the passenger seat.

"Why did you punch Leon?" the woman demanded.

"You said he was a tool!" protested Blood.

She gave him a tight smile. "It's no joke. He follows Takapa!" She turned to look at Kate with piercing pale blue eyes. "Chances are he wanted the girl for a good reason."

Kate felt a chill of fear. "What's going on here?"

Blood ignored her. "It's all right, Lydia," he assured his companion. "The girl's a peace offering. Insurance, if you like." He looked in the rearview mirror at Kate and gave a rueful smile. "You see, *she's* the one Takapa is after. Don't you think he'll forgive *me* my crimes if I deliver her direct to his door?"

Lydia considered for a moment, then settled contentedly in her seat. "You know, Adam," she said, "you might be right." She sounded amused. "And yes—Leon really is a *total* tool."

Kate put her hands to her temples. "No, this isn't happening."

Lydia laughed. Then she turned to Blood. "Okay, slow down. This is the place."

"The gathering's here, is it?" Blood pulled over to the side of the road. "No wonder they were catching up with our little runaway if she was scurrying about on their doorstep."

So that was where the 'wolves had been herding her: right back into Takapa's arms. But now it seemed her long-distance pen pal was going to do the job himself. Kate lunged for the door.

Blood flicked the central locking. "Stay still," he commanded, turning in his seat to face her. "And lie down, out of sight. We wouldn't want any Peeping *Toms* looking in on you now, would we?"

Had his stress on the word been deliberate or . . . ? Kate opened her mouth to speak, but Blood shook his head just a fraction. Trembling, she obediently lay facedown on the leather seating.

Lydia looked at Blood. "The gathering's due to start very soon. Are you coming up with her?"

"Not just yet," said Blood smoothly. "I wouldn't want to gate-crash your little lupine party. Besides, I want to get some answers out of the girl as to how she came to be loose on the streets. Why not call me when business is concluded and I'll march her up?" He leaned forward and kissed Lydia's cheek. "Oh, and don't tell a soul, will you? I want to make a big entrance."

"All right," Lydia agreed. "But you'd better park around the back. If Leon sees you here, he'll go nuts." Lydia pressed a perfectly made-up cheek against Blood's clean-shaven one, gave Kate an amused look, then slid out of the car. "Don't lose your little olive branch. . . . I'd hate to see you lose anything else as a result."

"Bye, then!" called Blood with mock jollity. Lydia slammed the car door shut behind her, and Blood drove away. "Great Gorgon knockers," he muttered, suddenly sounding a lot less refined. "I am *such* a bloody hero!"

"Yeah, you've so swept me off my feet." Kate felt sick with disappointment. She almost wished she was back in Takapa's freezing storeroom. "I just don't believe this. Are you 'wolf?"

"No."

"That blonde bitch is. She's your girlfriend?"

"Used to knock about with her, yeah. Scrubs up well, doesn't she?" All his elegance and charm had apparently slipped out of the car with Lydia. "I'm hoping we can maybe work things out."

Kate shook her head, feeling doubly betrayed. "You bastard. I've pictured us meeting up so many times over the last three years and I never once imagined—"

"Look, love, I think you'll find I saved your life."

She bristled. "Right. So you can save your own."

"Get down!" hissed Blood, pulling over at the side of the road. "They'll see you!"

Kate compromised on a half crouch. "How did you recognize me, anyway?"

"I didn't. But Lydia recognized that bloke Leon chasing you. And since he *was* chasing you and since Tom's gassed on a bit about—"

"Tom!" Kate jerked her head up, her long black hair whipping around her face. "What have you done with him, you—?"

"I sent him to Jicaque, just as you asked," said Blood angrily, switching off the engine.

"It's a trap! And all thanks to me." Kate started

kicking at the passenger door. "Let me out of here, you asshole."

"Just calm down and shut up a minute!"

"Unlock this door!" she shrieked, glaring wildly at him, tears of anger streaming down her face.

"I'm not going to hurt you," Blood yelled. Then something slammed down on the hood of the car, and his voice dropped in volume. "Er . . . but they might."

Two large men had leaned in on the car. They blocked the way forward, peering in through the windshield.

Kate lunged uselessly for the door again but recoiled as a hand slapped up against the window. Long talons began to tap out a slow, melancholic rhythm.

Then a gaunt, pale face pressed up against the tinted glass, a malicious smile twisting the all-too-familiar features. "Don't cry, little girl," said Marcie Folan. "Mommy's here."

# CHAPTER TWENTY

Tom was lying in a fetal position in the middle of Jicaque's red mat. Scented candles placed in and around the bronze statues cast a golden light throughout the entire room. The drug-tipped thorn had worked quickly, turning Tom's bones to mush.

He'd been stripped to the waist and gently wrapped up in the wolf skin. It clung to his sweating body. Now, with every breath of drowsy air, his senses swam a little deeper into a cold night that came for him alone.

Tom heard Tulung speak as though from a hundred miles away. "He is prepared, Professor. We can begin."

*Professor?* Tom wondered vaguely.

"Switch on the webcam," said Jicaque. He paused. "And signal to Takapa that we're ready when he is."

Tom felt the world fall away beneath him.

Jicaque couldn't have said that. No way.

The wolf pelt squeezed him still more tightly, like it was trying to drain the life from him. Tom wanted to scream out, but his tongue was like a fat slug leeching to his lips; he couldn't even open his mouth. He heard the synthesized chime of a PC starting up, tried to roll over onto his back, but it was like every limb had been pulverized.

A distorted image of the old man loomed over him, a hundred miles high. "Jicaque?" he croaked.

The old man shook his head. "My name is DeVries. I'm a professor." He smiled coldly. "And an enthusiast of amateur dramatics." He shrugged off his enormous wizard robes. Beneath them he was wearing the gown of a surgeon. A scalpel gleamed in one of his prune-skinned hands.

Tulung pointed the webcam down to where Tom lay, capturing everything for electronic posterity.

"Don't struggle, son," DeVries's voice rumbled. "Hold still and you won't feel a thing."

Kate stared at her mother's face, numb with shock. She jumped as a brief, sharp whizzing sound jolted through the car. "No, don't unlock the door!" she shrieked at Blood.

Too late.

Blood nodded to the men blocking their way and then jumped swiftly out of the car. Marcie Folan opened a rear door and reached inside. Kate yelled, kicking out at her. But Blood had opened the other rear door. He hauled Kate out of the car backward and twisted an arm behind her back.

She winced. "Let go of me!"

"Mrs. Folan, I presume?" Blood had jumped back into smooth-talking mode, extending a hand to Marcie. She looked at it like she might bite it off. "I'm Adam Blood. I've recaptured your wayward daughter."

"Have you indeed?" Marcie replied frostily.

Blood nodded, watching warily as Marcie's escorts slowly advanced on them. "As you can see, Kate is not very happy about it."

Kate felt like her insides were full of broken glass. "How did you find me?"

Marcie shrugged. "I was assured by Takapa that you'd be brought to me at the end of his gathering," she replied. "I'm his guest of honor, you know. I certainly wasn't expecting to find you out here." She looked pointedly at Blood.

"As I said," Blood assured her, "she got away, but I caught her again."

"I'd advise you, Mr. Blood," said Marcie quietly, her gaze fixed on Kate, "to hand my daughter over to me. I've come a very long way for her."

Kate felt Blood squeeze her hand. "Ordinarily, I'd love to," he said, "but I'm afraid I really must hand Kate over to dear old Papa Takapa myself. I'm currently in his bad books, you see. And as he does seem extremely interested in your daughter, my delivery of her might win his favor."

"Of course he's interested in *my* daughter," Marcie said haughtily. She took a step toward Kate, and Blood took one in retreat. "He wants the endorsement of my family name. If the Folans support him, others will, too. And I must say, his plans sound . . . exciting."

"He's insane, a maniac," Kate hissed. "You and he should get along fine."

Marcie ignored her. "All right, enough." She turned to Blood impatiently. "We don't want to make a spectacle outside, do we? Hand her over to me, Mr. Blood, and we'll all go and see Takapa together."

The two men escorting Marcie moved in behind Blood. Reluctantly he pushed Kate toward her mother.

Marcie grabbed hold of Kate like a dog snatching a bone. "You and that silverblood bastard killed my son," she whispered softly in Kate's ear.

"He was also my brother. And he was going to slaughter us both," Kate whimpered.

"You're going to pay. You and the boy. Over and over again." Marcie's sharp teeth bit at Kate's earlobe. She drew blood. "Did you honestly think there was anywhere in existence you could hide from me?"

"Where's Dad?" Kate demanded shakily.

"Back home. Grieving." Marcie shook her head. "He can't protect you any longer."

"Yes, well," Blood announced loudly. "It's this way in, isn't it?"

Blood led the party around to the front of the

conference center. Determined not to speak, not to cry, not to shake, Kate let her mother guide her through the dark double doors and into a nondescript reception room, empty of staff.

"Wait out here with Mr. Blood, please," Marcie said to one of her escorts. Then she looked at Blood coldly. "If you've lied to me about anything at all, you're dead."

Blood smiled sweetly. "Cheerio."

Kate was marched down the corridor. One of Marcie's escorts knocked smartly on a door.

"Enter."

It was Takapa's voice.

The aide opened the door and Marcie pushed Kate into the room. Takapa's pink eyes flashed her a look as cold and filthy as the storeroom she'd escaped from. He slipped a dark pin-striped jacket on over a shirt that was barely whiter than he was and gave a small bow to Marcie. "Mrs. Folan, it is an honor to meet you and to have you here today." He turned to Kate. "And here is your daughter. Apprehended as you instructed." There was no trace in his manner of the giggling depravity Kate had witnessed before.

"Having gone to such trouble to catch her, I'm surprised you let her slip away again so soon," said Marcie coolly.

Takapa looked suitably chastised. "I was soon alerted to her escape. My best agents rounded her up and brought her straight here." He reached out a hand to pet Kate's cheek, and she flinched. "To me."

Marcie seemed unimpressed. "A man called Blood claims to have caught her."

"Blood!" Now Takapa seemed amused. "Excellent. Our little redecoration of his apartment must've scared him even more than I'd hoped. Through him I got the boy too." He clapped softly. "Mrs. Folan, I want you to know that the woman responsible for Kate's escape has been caught and dealt with. She'll now be joining us at the post-gathering buffet." He showed his fangs in an unpleasant smile.

*So much for Patience and her "survivor" rant,* Kate thought darkly.

Marcie nodded, apparently satisfied. "And the boy? Tom Anderson?"

"Come through to the auditorium," said Takapa, "and you'll soon see."

Marcie nodded. "I hope I'm not going to be bored."

"I'm certain you won't." Takapa flicked the silver double helix that dangled from his ear and smirked.

Kate had seen that spiraling shape somewhere before . . . in some textbook somewhere. It clicked: biology. That double helix was a strand of DNA, the genetic code for all life, both human and lupine. But what was its importance to Takapa?

As he excused himself to prepare for his entrance, Kate and her mother were ushered from the room to a small auditorium. It was dark and smoky. Maybe fifty or sixty men and women were gathered inside, seated in neat rows. Even though they wore their human forms, a feral excitement hung like a heavy scent in the air.

Kate was forced to sit in a vacant chair near the back, the grip of her mother's hand like a vise around her wrist.

Spotlights in the ceiling began to glow. Takapa walked down the aisle and turned to face his audience. His angular body stood like a skeletal tree before a large, white-glowing screen, where Kate assumed some kind of presentation could be projected. The light was still dim, but Takapa blinked furiously like he was dazzled.

"I thank you all for being here," he called out, his words echoing around the auditorium. "I won't waste your time, for time is short for the whole of our kind. Unless you listen to me." He paused.

Kate caught whispers from the crowded rows around her.

"How much longer can we survive in the modern world?" Takapa questioned. "Man's ignorance, his superstitious fear, was once our greatest defense against him. Now his worship of technology, his refinement of reason, allows him no room for that fear."

"So?" someone shouted. "If he don't believe in us, we're safe."

"Safe?" Takapa shook his head. "You cling to the illusion of freedom. You're all too scared to see that we've shut ourselves away in the *enemy camp*. We squat in *man's* towns and cities and build for ourselves the best lives we can. We skulk in the houses *man* has made and only dare venture out to hunt at night—praying that *man's* eyes aren't upon us."

"Of course we've got to live that way," a woman called out. "For most of our lives, we're men and women too."

"We are *more* than men!" Takapa shouted. "More than women. Our secret community is not bound by man's laws, yet we are his prisoners." He stared about at the indifferent faces in the auditorium. "Don't you dream of warm, sweet nights? When you can hunt and kill and feast with only the full moon watching you?"

Kate heard her mother give a low sigh of pleasure.

"Hallelujah," called someone sarcastically. "He's peddling Wolf Time, brothers."

"Listen to me!" Takapa called over the jeers that followed. "Our community must unite! You dare not live in isolated pockets any longer. How long can you last with the human population ever expanding, devouring our woodlands, our fields, our hunting grounds?"

"If we band together, we just become a bigger target," someone else called, to scattered applause.

"*We* are hunters! We should not be the hunted!" Takapa almost shrieked. There was more applause, louder. "Our numbers must swell! *Humanity* must become our target."

"Turn the whole world 'wolf?" a heavyset man mocked. "They'd be mixed-blood mongrels!"

"Our history is sacred," yelled another.

"Our future is *more* sacred," Takapa argued. "But I'm not suggesting we start biting to turn as a general rule. We may turn a man's body, but not always his temperament. And that could breed a powerful enemy within." He raised his voice. "Yet through science, through man's own technology, we shall find an answer."

Kate looked nervously around the darkened auditorium. People were listening closely now, intrigued. Takapa was winning them over.

"Tell me, you who speak of our sacred past . . ." He flung out his stick-thin arms. "Who here knows of the Rituals of the Troubled Wolf?"

"There are seven of them." Marcie spoke out, her voice rattling around the room in hard echoes. "The healers devised them centuries ago to be used when the psychological balance between *were* side and wolf side shifts, causing mental conflict and possible damage to the physical health of the subject. Common in silverbloods." She glanced at Kate. "Especially common in werelings."

"Mrs. Folan," said Takapa with a deferential smile, "the reports of your medical knowledge are not exaggerated, I see. You're correct, of course. But people today, pumped full of food additives, hormones, and steroids, are poor meat for these rituals to work on. Success in unbinding the spirits of wolf and human so that the wolf may gain dominance is rare." He paused, pink eyes gleaming. "But now, science can take us further. It can actually identify what *makes* the werewolf—on a genetic level."

People were starting to heckle again: "Why?" "What for?"

Kate guessed that to these 'wolves, mixing modern technology with old traditions was sacrilege. To her, it was downright terrifying. But she saw that Marcie was staring at the screen expectantly.

"With this knowledge we can better understand our heritage," Takapa went on. "And this better understanding will help us to supplant the heritage of sterile humanity."

"It can't be done!" a woman called.

"If we unite under a strong leader with vision, it can!" Takapa signaled to someone at the back of the auditorium. The low lights dimmed further as the white screen behind him blurred into darkness and color. "What you're about to see is being broadcast live from a very special clinic across town."

An image formed, bleary but true.

Kate's stomach somersaulted and landed messily.

She was looking at Tom, lying motionless on a red mat. He was bound up in a wolf pelt, and an old man dressed in a surgeon's gown was crouched over him protectively, like a dog standing guard over food. He held a knife in his hand.

Kate tried to get up from her seat, but Marcie pulled

her back down and clamped a hand over her mouth.

"The boy is a wereling," said Takapa, pausing for effect.

Excited whisperings and mutterings began to fill the auditorium.

Takapa continued. "As you all know, a wereling's human self dominates his wolf. Through detailed analysis of his genetic makeup, *this* wereling will teach us much about the way human and wolf genes interact." There were more rumblings from the audience.

Takapa was clearly loving it.

His voice rose, his arms reached out, and Kate could see that he was playing the messiah. "It is written, of course, that a wereling heralds the coming of Wolf Time: a changeful boy who overthrows his human instincts to give himself to the wolf forever. A first sacrifice that spells doom for the human world." He laughed, a hollow, mirthless sound. "You may regard that as mere coincidence, of course, but I do not doubt you will find it fitting."

A few people were starting to leave, muttering in disgust about blasphemies and wasted time. But most remained, glued to the bleary visuals on the screen. Kate struggled in her mother's grip but was held firm.

"Through this broadcast I shall prove to you I am sincere in my intent to lead our race onto a new plateau in its evolution," proclaimed Takapa. "I shall prove that I have the necessary vision. And that I have the expertise at my command to make our wildest dreams possible. Professor Lucian DeVries of the Bruges chapter will now explain the procedure you are about to witness." He pulled a small clip-on microphone from his jacket pocket. "Professor?"

So Tom wasn't with Jicaque, Kate realized, no matter what Blood believed. Had he been tricked, just as Tom doubtless had?

The old man looked gravely into the camera and held a small microphone to his mouth. The crowd quieted to hear what he had to say. Clearly he was a man of fewer words than his boss. "I will begin the procedure at once," he said.

Tom rocked feebly, trying to break free of his bonds. His hands were trapped against his hips by the pelt, his mouth was dry, his vision flecked with red. He could hear the tinny sound of a man's voice from the PC, talking of werelings and science and the future, but he couldn't grasp the overall meaning. A thick fog seemed to fill his head.

Tulung was pointing a camera at the old man. He was droning on about insertions, bone scrapings, mutated DNA.

Tom knew he couldn't have long.

Renewing his efforts, he squirmed and wriggled on his back, trying to pull free of the wolf pelt. He looked down to find that something small and red had fallen from his jeans pocket.

The gris-gris Blood had given him.

As subtly as he could, he shifted his body until his face was next to the shriveled bundle. Inhaled. The stink, sulfuric and spiced, almost made him choke—but it started to cut through his cloudy senses, sharp as the knife in DeVries's hand.

In desperation he bit down on the withered chili. The hot, cloying taste flamed through him. As his consciousness cleared, panic threatened to overcome him. He gagged, spat out the charm, struggled more desperately.

"The subject is clearly becoming overwrought," he heard the professor say. "Tulung, subdue him once more, please."

"No!" shouted Tom. "You can't do this!"

"You can't stop us," said the old man gently.

Tom arched his back and kicked out at the old man. DeVries fell back against one of the statues, and the scalpel slipped from his hand.

As DeVries bawled for Tulung to put down the camera and help him, Tom fumbled for the knife. He couldn't get a proper grip, and the blade sliced into the soft flesh of his fingertips. He cried out with pain.

*Keep your anger,* Wesley had said. *That helps push it on.*

Tulung was coming for him with another thorn. Tom kicked him in the stomach, sent him sprawling back into a workbench.

As he watched Tulung recover to begin another advance, rage rose like bile in the back of his throat. He could feel the blood speeding through his veins, could feel his skin crawling and his insides quivering with anticipation. A familiar hunger burned through him, hot as the slashes scoring his fingertips.

"Subject is attempting transformation into the 'wolf state," the professor said calmly into his recovered microphone. "Given his nature and his drug-induced condition, the results may be unpredictable."

"Keep away from me, both of you!" Tom bellowed, drowning out the old man's voice. Then he shook his head and smiled as his senses shifted and darkened. What did DeVries know, anyway?

Tom wasn't attempting anything.

He was *becoming*.

The pelt of the wolf burst open with a dull ripping noise as Tom's body swelled in size. He groaned with pleasure as his spine broke and folded, as his hips ruptured and tipped him forward onto all fours.

But something was wrong. The sweet agony of the transformation refused to fade. The wolf inside him was only half out, still constrained. His blood boiled around bones that were fused stuck and solid in unnatural shapes. He yelped and screamed; the power to reason scraped away—only the power to feel remaining.

Tom saw Tulung and the professor advancing on him again. And he was powerless to fight back.

## CHAPTER TWENTY-ONE

Kate stared in horror at the screen as Takapa called out for calm. The camera had been put down somewhere now and showed a frantic, twisted figure on its knees, shaking and screaming in the middle of the room.

Its doglike front legs ended in clenched fists; its back was bent and deformed; its head hung down to the floor. Kate was glad its face was hidden. She couldn't bear to see Tom's eyes looking out from this poor deformed, mutant creature.

"The wereling appears to be caught midway through transformation," came the professor's fascinated commentary over the loudspeakers. "The rituals have impeded full metamorphosis. This hybrid form is ungainly, nonresponsive—"

"Sedate him!" yelled Takapa into his microphone. "Quickly! Harvest the mutated DNA. It could prove invaluable to our research!"

"Leave him alone!" Kate shrieked. "Don't do it!"

"You see what I can do?" Takapa roared at his

audience; then a few childish giggles escaped his thin lips. "My science gives me absolute mastery over human and wolf. As nature binds them together, so *I* can tear them apart!"

"Stop this!" Kate lunged forward. She wanted to reach out to Tom, to smash Takapa, to tear down the viewing screen and destroy this sick spectacle. "You twisted, murdering sack of—"

Marcie hauled Kate back and cuffed her hard around the face, stunning her into silence. Then she stood, shouting over the astonished din that was building in the auditorium. "Once you have these cells, are you through with the boy?"

Takapa stared at her as if affronted. "Mrs. Folan, I feel—" He broke off, composed himself once more. "Excuse me for a few moments, my friends," he announced to the baffled crowd. "And meantime . . . enjoy the show."

The screen showed the old professor advancing on Tom's prone body. His voice echoed out over the crowd's mutterings. "I'm ready to take the first sample."

Takapa hurried over. "Mrs. Folan, I had hoped we could discuss the boy's fate once my demonstration was completed. It's vital that my audience—"

"I am part of your audience," said Marcie briskly, "and I've seen and heard enough. You have my support, Takapa. We can talk details later."

A smug smile twitched at Takapa's lips. He

looked hungrily at Kate, pink eyes glistening. "I welcome that discussion."

"All in due course," snapped Marcie. "Now where's the boy?"

"Nearby. But I'm afraid I have no transportation to spare—"

"Blood can take us in his car," Marcie said flatly.

Takapa shrugged and nodded. "Well, he should know the address. I faked a message from one of his contacts and fed it through to him."

Kate bit her lip. So Blood *hadn't* realized he was sending Tom into a trap. Still, his betrayal of her had been real enough.

"I must insist, however," Takapa went on, "that the professor carries out his work without interruption."

"Oh, the professor may *begin* carving the boy," hissed Marcie. "But *I* want to finish it."

Kate looked up anxiously at the screen, her stomach twisting. Tom was rocking back and forth in silence as the long-haired man and the professor bent over him.

"Don't worry, Kate. You won't miss a thing." Marcie smiled. "You'll see all the action. Up close. In the flesh."

Tom offered little resistance as Tulung knelt on the back of his neck, forcing his face down against the floor. He felt a scratch on his cheek. One of the drug-tipped thorns fell to the floor beside him.

Something sharp entered Tom's back. He

bucked, tried to lash out, but Tulung held his upper body fast. His front limbs were pinned to the floor, though he could barely move them anyway.

*You're finished,* he thought. *This is how it ends. You die in some rented flat in New Orleans, a misshapen monster, cut apart by 'wolf maniacs.*

He growled, struggled to shift Tulung's bulk, snapped his teeth.

*You lost Kate. You let her down when she needed you.*

"Don't fight, my boy."

*Now she'll wind up raped or dead, and you did nothing. Nothing except get yourself killed.*

"It will only hurt more if you fight," insisted DeVries.

But Tom couldn't feel any more pain than he did thinking about Kate.

With a roar so deep and loud it was almost deafening, he reared up and shook Tulung clear. The big man was hurled through the air, crashed heavily into one of the workbenches, and the camera he had placed there tumbled to the floor with him.

The knife, or the needle, or whatever the hell it was pushed deeper into Tom's back. He howled but welcomed the pain. It was poking, pricking, stabbing his consciousness back to life.

And giving it over to the wolf.

"You're our designated driver, Blood," Marcie snapped as she breezed out of the auditorium with

246

Kate in tow. "Take us to the place you sent the boy."

Blood blinked in surprise and turned to the man guarding him, as if hoping for an explanation. "I'm not sure what you're talking about."

"You were given a fake address by Takapa," she snapped, "purporting to have come from one of your friends."

Blood stared at her and opened his mouth like he was about to swear loudly. Then he swept a hand over his face as if to wipe clean his expression and was smiling, smooth and assured once more. "I knew it was fake. Blake's out of town, out of contact. But I played along. Like I say, if I want to survive in this city, I need protection."

"So you've sold your soul to Takapa," Kate said coldly.

Blood looked at Marcie. "How did she wind up so melodramatic?"

"Drive me to that address or you're dead," Marcie hissed.

"Ask a stupid question." Blood sighed.

He allowed the guard to lead him outside to his car, and soon he, Kate, Marcie, and her escort were under way.

They drove in silence. On the backseat Kate could feel her mother trembling in anticipation beside her.

"What's happening to the kid there, anyway?" Blood wondered.

"Like you care," said Kate sourly.

"You can come up and see for yourself," Marcie told him. She lightly patted Kate's leg and leaned in to her. "Remember poor Mark?"

Kate said nothing.

Marcie licked her lips. "This one's going to be so much messier."

"Please, it's not like it was with Mark." Hot tears forced themselves from Kate's eyes. "I'll let him turn me. I swear I won't run away again. I'll let you do what you want."

"That's thoughtful of you, honey," Marcie said coldly. "But you should know I'll do that anyway."

Kate clutched hold of her mother's hand. "Please don't kill him."

Marcie swatted her away. "You belong to Takapa now."

Kate almost retched. "You can't be serious."

"He has no breeding, of course, but big ideas. And he's not afraid to act, unlike so many of those weakling 'wolf fools." She smiled. "Perhaps it's punishment enough to let him have you."

"Er, we're here," Blood announced awkwardly, pulling to the side of the road. "Top apartment."

Marcie turned to Kate. Her eyes flashed yellow. "After you."

The human part of Tom silently slipped away as the wolf overcame him. His twisted bones ground into true forms, strong and efficient. His trembling flesh became packed with muscle, and he groaned as warm, fresh strength poured through them. His snout grew longer, his teeth sharpened along with his vision. And he could smell another 'wolf close by.

Not the man with the knife. He was backing away, terrified.

It was Tulung. He'd shrugged off his human form like it was dirty laundry and now hunkered down, ready to spring. He made a massive wolf, barrel-chested, the hunched body rippling with powerful muscles and covered in rich, graying fur.

A bell was ringing. It came from the door. But to Tom it served as a signal for the battle to begin.

"No reply." Blood shrugged, taking his finger off the doorbell. "Maybe they went out for a pizza or something."

"Or they're all dead," Kate murmured shakily.

"Possibly," Blood conceded weakly, pulling off his jacket.

Kate saw that his pale blue shirt was soaked with sweat.

Marcie swore. "There must be a back way in."

The guard herded Kate and Blood after Marcie as she ventured down an alleyway.

"Fire escape," Marcie observed. Then she smiled at Kate and corrected herself. "*No* escape."

The battle was brutal and dirty. The two 'wolves piled into each other, biting and clawing, anger and hate driving them on to greater and greater violence.

Tom broke clear of Tulung and strayed too close to the old man. A shriveled hand darted out at him with a knife. Tom turned and snapped at the old man's fingers, crunching through brittle bones. The sound of screaming rang in his ears, drove him away.

Tom tasted blood in his mouth, what he craved. Why was it making him feel so sick? Suddenly he was being grappled to the ground, huge claws scraping at his chest. He sank his teeth into Tulung's shoulder, tore ravenously at the thick flesh. But his opponent bit back, harder, sharper. Jagged teeth sliced into his neck. Dots of crimson misted his vision.

"Lucifer's arse," swore Blood as Marcie threw open the back door of the apartment. "What the hell . . . ?"

Kate took in the scene in frightened flashes: splashes of blood on the wall. The old man wailing, clutching his hand. Tom, fully 'wolf now, all clothes torn away. His sleek body was locked in combat with a massive gray-black beast, rolling over and over through the trashed apartment.

She ran forward, but the guard yanked her back by her wrist. "Tom!" she yelled.

He turned to face her, his brown eyes wide and afraid.

The other 'wolf, seeing Tom distracted, sank its jaws into his neck. Tom collapsed under its weight, howling.

"Leave him, you idiot!" Marcie shrieked. "He's mine."

The attacking beast paid her no heed.

Marcie seized a large curved dagger from a bench top and in a moment slit the gray-black 'wolf's throat wide open. The hulking creature spasmed, then fell heavily backward, a bloody foam gushing from its wound.

"Tulung," sobbed the old surgeon, reaching out, his ruined hand still leaking blood.

Marcie kicked him hard in the face. He fell back, silenced.

Kate saw that Tom was still alive. He lay panting weakly, staring up at his savior.

She held her breath.

"Now for you, you little bastard," Marcie spat.

"Mom, no!" Kate screamed, struggling against the guard holding her back.

But her mother was already changing. Her hands curled into claws. Her spine was gnarling, hunching over. A terrible roar was building in her chest. Spittle splashed out of her open mouth.

Kate shut her eyes, wished she could block her ears as the snarls grew louder and louder. Then stopped, with a loud, ringing thud.

She opened her eyes to see Marcie lying face-down on the floor and Blood standing over her, wielding a heavy paperweight.

"Now just shut the bloody hell up!" he told her lifeless body.

Kate was thrown aside by the guard. She fell against the wall and banged her head. The guard pulled a gun from a shoulder holster hidden beneath his jacket and aimed it at Blood's head.

A cell phone started ringing, playing "God Save the Queen" at earth-shattering volume.

Instinctively the guard looked behind him at the source of the sound.

Blood swung the paperweight up again in a wide arc. It connected with the underside of the guard's jaw, knocking his head back. He went down like the proverbial ton of bricks. The gun fired, and a bronze statue rang with the bullet's impact.

Stunned, Kate pulled the cell phone from Blood's abandoned jacket and hit okay. A woman's voice whined out from the receiver.

"Adam, are you there? It's Lydia. This gathering is *so* over as far as I'm concerned. It's not even a funny joke. Everyone's leaving and . . . Adam? Hello?"

"He'll call you back," Kate said, and disconnected.

Blood was staring in a kind of distressed wonder at the bodies littering the floor. "Jesus, I *am* a hero," he muttered incredulously.

"I thought you were the biggest, most traitorous bastard in the whole world," Kate informed him.

The paperweight slipped from Blood's hand and clattered to the floor. "If you had only shut up for a minute back in the car and let me explain, I'd have told you I was trying to rescue you. But I couldn't let Lydia know that was the reason I'd clobbered her friend, could I?"

Kate decided Blood's real, rougher accent suited him better. "I guess not," she agreed, rubbing the back of her head. She pushed past him to get to Tom, who was just lying there, prone in his 'wolf state.

"Still, it's probably just as well," Blood decided wearily. "You having a tantrum like that in the car helped convince your old mum I was on her side. Or at least, looking out for myself."

"Enough about you," Kate grumbled, pressing her fingers against the dark fur on Tom's neck, soaked with saliva.

"Is he okay?" Blood asked seriously.

"I'm not sure." The warm pulse under Kate's fingers was ragged and erratic.

"He's still breathing; I suppose that's something," said Blood dubiously. "But so is your mum. I don't think I hit her hard enough." He gestured to the gun on the floor. "We could always . . ."

Kate turned and shook her head fiercely. "No. We're not like her."

"I'm only being practical—" He took a sudden breath. "My God . . ."

"What is it?" asked Kate sharply, scrambling to her feet.

"Tom. He's changing back."

She watched the werewolf body, slumped on its front, as it writhed and shrank back into hairless, human form. "He's going to be all right," she whispered, clutching Blood's arm in relief.

Tom was covered in cuts and bruises, there was an evil gash above his left eye, and he looked dreadful. But he was, undeniably, alive. Kate grabbed a crumpled, colorful cloak from the floor and laid it over him.

Tom rolled over and his eyes focused on her. "Kate . . . you're okay?"

"I'm fine," she assured him. "Great, in fact." She gave him an exaggerated wink. "Semicolon-dash-right parenthesis."

He smiled drowsily. "It's all so hazy. What the hell happened here?"

She crouched down beside him and took his hand. "I think we won."

"Tom, you ungrateful sod!" cried Blood, picking up a scrap of white leather with a look of horror. "That's the last time I lend you a pair of my shoes!" He grinned. "Now pick yourself up, sharpish. Am I the only person who could really use a group hug right now?"

Kate fell into a clumsy embrace with the two of them for a few seconds, giggling and sobbing with the sudden rush of relief. As she pulled away, her fingers brushed over the smooth skin of Tom's bare neck. For a second everything else in the room fell away. Kate felt like no one was there but the two of them.

Before she could get a grip on how she really felt about that, her foot caught a wire and a furious voice screeched tinnily from the overturned PC.

"DeVries! You've ruined everything, DeVries! Answer me, what's happening there?"

Takapa.

While Blood helped Tom into the cloak, Kate scooped up the little microphone she'd seen the professor speak into. "The professor and his pal have met with a slight accident," she said. "Kiss your experiment goodbye, you pink-eyed freak."

In the PC monitor, lying on its side, she saw the live streaming video of him, standing alone in the auditorium. The picture was grainy and low resolution, but there was no mistaking the fury clouding his ugly face. "Later, freak. We are *so* outta here," she said. Then she ripped the microphone lead from its socket and switched off the monitor. Static crackled as a beady blackness closed its big square eye.

In the distance sirens were sounding. Coming their way.

"Let's get out of here," Tom said.

"Uh-huh." Kate nodded. "And go where?"

"Anywhere," said Tom, surveying the bloody carnage in the room. He reached out and squeezed her hand. "Anywhere but here."

## Chapter Twenty-Two

That evening Kate and Tom waited together in Bloodlettings' New Orleans office while the owner crashed around in a back room, apparently tidying up a few bits of outstanding business.

Blood ran back into the main office. "You might find this interesting. One of my pals reckons he really has found Jicaque's address."

Tom groaned, pulled his borrowed sweater up over his head.

"And it's not a trick?" Kate asked.

"I spoke with him myself," Blood replied. "It's not Takapa hacking into his e-mail account like last time. I doubt that albino could hack his way out of a wet paper bag after his demonstration disaster. His name will be mud as far as the lupine community's concerned. At least until he can come up with something a bit more convincing."

Tom looked dubious. "So this lead is on the level?"

"I'll drive you there myself," Blood offered. "Then I'm on my way."

"You're leaving?" Tom and Kate chorused together.

Blood shrugged. "If Takapa's name is mud, mine must be absolute shit. Not even Lydia's talking to me. So I'm going away until things calm down round here."

"I'm sorry," Tom muttered. "If we'd never come here—"

"Forget it," Blood assured him. "I've not had a holiday in three years; I'm looking forward to it. And thanks to you, I've actually cleaned up a bit of this city's dirt instead of just watching and whining on about how god-awful it all is." He smiled. "Maybe now I *can* move on. But first things first."

"Jicaque?" Kate asked.

"No," Blood replied. "I need to know: in your e-mails, why the hell did you call yourself 'Troll Lover'?"

She smiled. "First, because I'm totally indifferent to trolls, so no one would connect me with that name. Second, and more importantly, because the name suggests some kind of intriguing deviancy that makes weirdos like you more willing to help me out."

Blood looked at Tom. "Devious little cow, isn't she?"

Tom nodded. "But smart."

"Just get the car," said Kate with a smile.

They drove to the address in the French Quarter. Dusk was starting to creep in on the city. Tom felt like eyes were on them everywhere they turned.

"It's up on the next right," Blood announced.

Kate looked at Tom and held up crossed fingers.

"This neighborhood looks familiar," Tom said as they slowed to a halt. "I think I wandered through here after I—" His guts twisted with sudden recognition. "Oh no. It's that place there, isn't it?"

The car had parked outside an old run-down movie theater. A faded sign read CINEMA MEDIN.

Blood checked a piece of paper. "This is the place. But an old movie theater? *Medin, Medin . . .*" He frowned. "Sounds like it's French."

"But it's not; it's meaningless," Kate swore. "No, not meaningless. It's a clue. *Cinema Medin.* An anagram of 'medicine man.'"

"No one likes a smart-arse, love," chided Blood. But he was smiling.

"Look. Above the entrance." Tom pointed to a large, grimy window that overlooked the faded billboard. A banner there advertised MANDRAKE'S, ALTERNATIVE DIET SPECIALISTS. "A health food store."

"Just like the rumors said," Kate breathed. "Then this *is* the place."

"I went inside that movie theater," Tom muttered softly. "There was a weird old guy in there, Inuit or something."

Kate stared at him. "But that must've been *him!* Jicaque himself! What did you—?"

"How was I supposed to know!" Tom yelled. "He freaked me out; I ran away! The place was full of rats!"

"Maybe that's his alternative diet," suggested Blood unhelpfully. "How about we go in? Maybe you can see him all over again."

Cautiously they left the car and got in through the old movie theater's open fire door. Nothing stirred in the gloom. As they moved farther into the building, Tom stepped on something.

The bloated body of a decapitated rat.

Kate screwed up her nose. "Someone's been here before us."

"Your mom?" Tom wondered.

"My pal says she hasn't left Takapa's place since she got away from that apartment," Blood reminded him.

Kate snorted. "She can still tell others what to do, can't she?"

They pressed on, though Tom had a fair idea of what they'd find when they reached the apartment above the theater.

Sure enough, the way through was well signed by kicked-down doors. Mandrake's was a shambles, turned over from top to bottom as thoroughly as Blood's office.

A message had been spelled out in rat entrails on

a splintered teak table. A crude little stunt, but the hairs rose on the back of Tom's neck just the same as his eyes flicked over it.

YOU'RE DEAD—SOON

"Jicaque," mused Blood, "or us?"

"Your mom must've known we'd come here," Tom said quietly. "She must've known that I still had hopes of finding a cure. So they got here first and took it."

"I don't know." Kate rattled some empty hangers in a closet. "Jicaque's clothes are all gone; all his potions and lotions too. I think maybe he knew they were coming for him and got away in time."

"Speaking of which," Blood said, checking through the window for any signs they were being watched, "I think it's time I got the hell out of here myself."

Blood took them to a newly converted warehouse apartment out in Gretna. Back at the Bloodlettings office he left them a bundle of keys, told them to take their pick of his properties until they figured out what to do next. He also insisted that they take five hundred dollars for new clothes and essentials.

"I never thought you'd wind up my sugar daddy." Kate grinned.

"I never thought I'd wind up a troll lover," he deadpanned.

"But you've done so much for us already," Tom said. "We can't take your money like this."

"You'd better," Blood told him. "I'm damned if I'm lending you any *more* of my clothes. Go and get your own."

Tom smiled. "Thanks." He offered Blood his hand.

"I told you to thank me when this was over," Blood replied. "And it's not. Not by a long way." But he shook hands just the same, kissed Kate on the cheek, then gathered up his luggage. "Tomorrow is the first day of the rest of your life," he said thoughtfully. "I always thought that saying was bollocks. But you know, there might just be something in it. Don't you think?"

With that, he turned on his heel with his bulky suitcases and left.

The apartment seemed like a different place once he'd gone: its bare white walls like bone, its clean, modern lines unwelcoming and severe.

Kate dumped the bundle of house keys on an ultracool but hopelessly uncomfortable couch and perched herself beside them. She started scrutinizing the tags.

"Where do you want to stay?" she asked Tom. "Lafayette, Vermilionville . . . ?"

"We can't linger here, that's for sure." Tom sighed as he flopped down beside her. "Your mom will be better soon and *really* out for blood. The 'wolves will be hunting us wherever we go."

"And we'll be hunting Jicaque," Kate murmured. "We'll get you cured, Tom. We will."

Tom wanted to believe it could be true. "We'll see," he said. "I just wish . . ."

*. . . that you'd kiss me,* he thought.

*. . . that I had the guts to kiss you.*

*. . . that all this horror wasn't the only thing keeping us together.*

"What do you wish?" Kate asked him.

Tom smiled and shrugged. "Doesn't matter."

Through the window the sky was violet as the sun sank beneath the low-rise skyline. Soon the moon would hold court over the city once again. Tom wondered what the days and nights ahead would hold for them. "Do you think we'll ever feel safe again?" he asked.

Kate half smiled. "Remember when my mother made me dress up and pose for you on the couch back home?"

"Yes," Tom replied quietly. She had been beautiful then. But she was even more beautiful to him now, with her ripped jeans and smudged face. The eyes . . . Her eyes were the same, pale green and haunted. "It feels like such a long time ago."

Kate looked at him. "Even with all the fear and the uncertainty . . . with all the running I know we'll have to do . . . I feel a million times safer here on this dumb, uncomfortable couch with you now. So that's got to be a good thing, right?"

Tom decided to take a chance. He took one of Kate's hands in his own. She didn't move it away. He smiled. "Right," he agreed.

They sat together in the darkening apartment, waiting for night to fall.